interVENTion

by

JHORDYNN

EDITED BY MADE 4 THIS™ (318) 406-2249

COVER DESIGNED AND FORMATTED BY
SUNNY GIOVANNI

PUBLISHED BY MADE 4 THIS™

COPYRIGHT © 2019. ALL RIGHTS RESERVED

ISBN: 978-0-578-54169-3

Made 4 This, LLC

AUTOGRAPHED BOOKS AVAILABLE ON JHORDYNN.COM

FOLLOW JHORDYNN ON FACEBOOK: JHORDYNN

FOLLOW JHORDYNN ON INSTAGRAM: jhordynn_writes

SUBSCRIBE TO JHORDYNN'S YOUTUBE: JHORDYNN

SUBSCRIBE TO JHORDYNN'S WEBSITE: JHORDYNN.COM

NEED HELP WRITING A BOOK OR ANYTHING ELSE? MY
COMPANY MADE 4 THIS CAN HELP YOU. CALL 318-406-
2249, OR EMAIL YOUR QUESTIONS AND NEEDS TO
BEASTEINC@GMAIL.COM

Thank you, Yahweh for giving me a strong and necessary message to spread. Mental health is an issue in my communities—Black and Christian—that is not properly addressed or treated. Thank you for getting the glory in my daughter's condition. Thank you for covering her, hiding her, protecting her, healing her. Thank you for allowing her to have Dandy Walker and hydrocephalus, but they not having her. Your strength is made perfect in my weakness. Whether I live or die, I belong to you.

Thank you, David for continuing to push me. Thank you for riding with me through every insane venture and idea that I come up with. Thank you for accepting that I am an artist with an artist's spirit—free and carefree. Thank you for never making me feel like I have to apologize for being me. Thank you for the greatest earthly gift anyone could give me: our daughter.

Thank you, Sugafoot for showing me life in another way. Your existence has shown me what love really means. Your existence has shown me what having faith really means. You are my chain—you help me grow. God has allowed me to create beautiful songs, poems, books, stories... but the greatest creation that He allowed me to birth is you.

Thank you, Me for doing it scared. Thank you for coming into your own. Thank you for every attempt at everything. You cannot succeed at that which you do not try. With shaking knees and a trembling voice, you are trying it all. Thank you.

THANK YOU TO MY SUPPORTERS!!! Y'all NEVER let me rest, sleep, break, NOTHING! THANK YOU FOR THAT! With every book that I release, you make it a bigger premier than the last. Every day, one of you inbox me on FB, telling me how my book(s) have helped or inspired you. I be minding my own business, chilling, and one of you will ask me, "When can I expect the next one?" LOL. Thank you. Y'all keep me going. For real.

Thank you, Julia for your pregnant belly. You came through for the visual God gave me for the cover. When CJ gets here, I will thank him, too.

Thank you, Mij for being my nephew (my first born, my first experiment) and for being on the book cover. I can only imagine what you were thinking as you were balled up on the floor, posing. You have been great ever since God knit you together in your mother's womb. Don't let NO ONE tell you differently.

Whew... here it goes.

interVENTion

Chapter 1

Green-eyed Monster

inter~~VENT~~<u>VENT</u>~~ion~~

"Aniyah, not tonight!" my neighbor yells at me through her door.

"Oh, yes, tonight! If you don't want me at your door every night, then you tell your fast ass daughter to leave my son alone! He has a full paid scholarship to any college of his choice. He is the star football player of his high school. She is a groupie looking for an opportunity!

"I am not blind, stupid, or dumb! She is trying to get pregnant by him to trap him. No, Ma'am! She got the right one! I ain't with this!"

LaTrice opens the door, "Aniyah, take your medicine."

"I don't need no medicine. Give your hot ass daughter Lyric some medicine. She's only sixteen, trying to get a baby by my son. I read them texts. She ain't trapping my baby!"

"Then let me see the texts, Aniyah," Trice tells me.

"I don't have his phone on me."

"Elijah! Get out the car and show me where my daughter has been texting you!" LaTrice yells out to my son.

I turn around and look at my car; he never comes out. Silently, I pleaded for him to come out the car, but he never did.

"Just tell your daughter to stay away and stop texting him."

"I will. And you stay away from my house, Aniyah."

"My pleasure."

I walk back to my car and drive off.

"These fast ass girls will try to catch you up every time. Everybody is looking for a come up. You are only fifteen with a full paid scholarship; girls think that you are their come up. Don't fall for that, Elijah. Listen to your mama. Your mama loves you and is always looking out for you."

"Yes, Ma'am," he answers.

"As a Black boy in this world, being good enough ain't good enough. Being perfect will get you *halfway* there. You have to be four times as good as your White competition.

"I said all that to say: no babies! You don't need any distractions or negative marks on your record. No babies, no baby mamas, nothing less than As on your report cards. You are headed for the top. You have to be better than the best. You have to be *It*."

"I understand, Mama. I'm doing everything you told me to and staying away from everything you warned me about. Stop worrying. I'mma make it," he tells me.

inter~~VENT~~ion

We arrive home.

"Go upstairs and bathe. When you come back down, dinner will be ready. I love you, Son."

"I love you, too, Ma."

My husband leans in for a kiss, but I dodge it.

"Really, Niyah?"

"Montrel, I need your help around here. I am doing it all for Elijah by myself, and I am starting to get tired. No. I *been* tired! I take him to all of his football practices, football games, take him to school, pick him up from school, take him to choir rehearsal at church. I could go on and on. Can you please help?"

"No. You chose to do this. If you are tired, stop. But don't put this on me. I want no parts of that bullshit."

"Your son's progress is bullshit?!"

"You heard exactly what I said, Aniyah. I ain't helping you with shit that has to do with Elijah. Don't ask me no more."

"I didn't make him by myself, Montrel!"

"Are you done?" he asks me.

"He is your son, too!" I yell.

"Anything else?" he asks.

I sigh and say, "No. We're done."

"Can we make love tonight?" he has the audacity to ask me.

"Not at all. If you want it, use your hand."

"This is bullshit, too! You are my wife, and I haven't touched you in years."

"Because I'm so consumed with Elijah. I'm doing this by myself! Help, and I would have room for sex."

"Once again, are you done?" he asks me.

"Yep," I answer.

"Good night," he tells me.

"You didn't even speak to your son when he came through the door!"

"I have nothing to do with him. How many times do I have to tell you that?"

"No more. I got it this time."

"Good night, again, Niyah."

"Good night."

Elijah comes downstairs for his dinner.

"I don't know how much of that you heard, but just know that nothing is wrong with you. I married the wrong man. He's just jealous of you because you are living out your dreams, and he never followed his."

"But I've done nothing wrong. I've done everything you have told me to do. I go to school, make good grades, be the best football player I can be, stay out of trouble, and stay away from girls. I have done nothing to that man!" Elijah says.

"Envy is a green eyed monster, Elijah. You don't have to do nothing but be yourself for people to be jealous of you. That's all you've done. And you're doing a great job. Keep it up. I'm proud of you."

interVENTion

Chapter 2

No Days Off

inter~~inter~~VENT~~ion~~

Four thirty a.m. comes so soon. I look over at my husband who is getting the best sleep of his life. I don't understand how his snoring hasn't woke him up. I look at the pillow that I just raised up from and contemplate placing it over his face until he stops squirming. But God is going to let him reap everything he's ever sowed, so I shake the thought and go on with my day.

Elijah has to be at school at six a.m. for football practice. I iron Elijah's and my clothes, bathe, then wake him up. While he showers, I do my hair and make-up. I go downstairs to cook breakfast. He always finishes getting ready at the same time that breakfast is ready. We eat breakfast together, brush our teeth together, and head out the door.

This is the routine every morning, Monday through Friday.

"Are you excited about your birthday party?" I ask him on the drive to school.

"No. Nobody came last year. Not a single soul."

"Well, that's because your birthday and Christmas are so close together. But for this year, I am throwing your party three weeks early, and I have sent out invitations eight months in advance. I send out a reminder invitation every week through emails and texts. This is your sweet sixteen. No one is going to miss it. I have made sure everyone can make it. People *will* be there this year. I can feel it."

inter~~inter~~VENT~~ion~~

We arrive at his school, and I park.

"Mama, please don't come with me."

"Yes, I'm coming. I need to see Lyric to make sure she doesn't try to trap you."

"Mama, I don't need you to do that. I can make my own decisions. Not like she can rape me. She's not a threat; she's not a problem. Please. Not today. You've already threatened her last week at practice. And you're always at her house. You're going to end up in jail for harassment. Especially because she's a minor.

"Her mama hasn't pressed charges, yet because y'all used to be best friends. But if you keep messing with her daughter, she won't care what y'all used to be. No more, Mama, okay? You're the only parent there this early. Go home. Go to sleep. It's early. Rest."

"No. Let's go," I tell him.

As we're walking onto the field, his football coach meets me at the bleachers.

"Mrs. Brent. You cannot step foot on this field. We have been instructed by Lyric's mom and the principal to call the police on you if you do or say anything to Lyric. Please leave. Now."

I see Lyric on the sideline, practicing her cheer. Cheerleaders are always whores. She ain't fooling me, and this ain't over.

"Now," Coach Ebarb reinforces.

I decide to walk away. Elijah has a huge game tonight that I cannot miss due to being in jail behind a thirsty teenage slut.

"Go, Number Four! You are amazing!" I yell at Elijah, as I walk away.

interVENTion

Chapter 3

Drinking About You

"These bills are out of control," Montrel tells me. "You have to get a job *now*. Reopen your business. Sell your ass. I don't give a damn! I can't foot it by myself no more. We have blown through savings and investments. We ain't even fifty. You want me to go back to slanging? Cuz I will!"

"If you helped me with Elijah, I would be able to work. I am doing all this by myself. So, you can pay the bills by yourself. Even trade."

"Since Elijah's extracurricular activities are making us poor, take him out of every fucking thang that you enrolled him in. Secondly, you can't get a job because you are drunk all the time, Aniyah!"

"I am *never* drunk!"

"Aniyah, you're drunk right now. And it's only six fifteen in the morning. You are sweating tequila, and the empty bottle is in the sink. A bottle that was full last night."

"Elijah drunk it."

Montrel lets out a laugh. "Not your sweet, innocent, does-nothing-wrong Elijah."

"Yes, him," I exhale. "I don't want to throw Elijah under the bus by lying on him, but I am left with no choice."

"So, Elijah drunk it, and it's coming out of your pores? You're a liar, Aniyah. Which is also how I know you're a drunk. You only lie when your lips are moving. I have to go to work so that I can afford gas to go back to work. Bye."

"Elijah has a game tonight, Montrel. Get off in time to go."

"Is he going to be able to play while he is drunk?" he sarcastically asks.

"Come out to the game and see, Montrel."

"Fuck you and that game."

He slams the door behind him. Happy that he's gone so I can pour myself a drink, I walk behind him to lock it. But my joy is shortened when I see LaTrice walking to Montrel. They engage in what is obviously a deep conversation. He turns around, looks at me through the window, shakes his head, and continues his conversation. He gives her a nod, a one-armed hugged, and drives off.

Her daughter Lyric wants my son, and she wants my husband. She can have him.

I open the door before she has the chance to knock.

"I didn't come here to start no mess, Niyah."

"You just lied," I say.

"No. Niyah, I love you. You were my best friend growing up. We are neighbors because we couldn't be apart. We both got married and still had to be houses apart. We had to drive the same vehicles. We even got pregnant together."

"Get to the point, Trice."

"I love you, and I miss you. I just want you to take your medicine. I want you to get help. I want you to be better. You are still my best friend. You just can't keep carrying on like this. I choose my daughter's safety and well-being over your freedom. I will press charges if you harass her one more time. You are a parent. You understand."

"Are you done?" I ask her.

"Aniyah, Elijah is—"

I snap my neck to her, buck my eyes, flare my nose, and dare her to finish her statement. "What is he, LaTrice? What is he?!"

She slowly walks backwards. "I've never met a young man like him. So sweet and full of life. I just want you to be okay. My Godson Elijah is not the problem; you are. Stay away from Lyric, and we'll be fine. Good bye."

I pull a glass out of the cabinet to pour liquor in, but decide to ditch the glass and down the bottle. Within four gulps, a bottle of Moscato is gone.

When I wake up from my nap, I realize that I have overslept. It's after four p.m., and I hadn't picked up Elijah from school at three fifteen. In a staggering panic, I search for my keys. I flip mattresses, look under rugs, ramshack drawers trying to find them. I hear my keys rattling.

"Looking for these?" Montrel asks, dangling my keys in front of me.

"Yes," I nearly cry. "I have to pick up Elijah."

"No. You're drunk."

"Please," I beg. "You're not going to do it."

"Enough is enough. No more, Aniyah. Your obsession with Elijah has gone too far."

"I'm not obsessed. I'm a mother. I'm just a mother who loves her son. Her only son that God has given her. Her son that she prayed so hard for ever since she was seven. A mother who just wants the best for her son. I'm just a mother who can't live without her son."

I see Montrel begin to soften, and his grip on my keys change from tormenting to protecting.

"It's not safe for you to drive. But isn't today game day, which means that the school is taking him to his game after school?"

I sigh a huge sigh of relief, "Yes. Yes. Yes. You are right. I didn't miss picking him up after school because the school is taking him to the game. I just need to go to the game to see him play."

"Call a cab," Montrel tells me.

"I will."

****

"Look at Number Four go!" I yell from the stands. "Go, Elijah! Run, Baby!"

I see Lyric there, cheering for the "team", but I know she's really cheering for Elijah. I will make sure he comes straight home tonight after the game. There will be no celebrating with the team. I don't trust her. I trust him, but I also know that he's a hormonal teen. I'm not taking the chance.

"He's open, Elijah! Tackle him!" I yell.

"What number is your son?" a lady asks me.

"Number four."

"I don't see a number four."

"It's dark out here. But I know my son. He's the one scoring."

"Oh! Well, congratulations. You must be proud."

"I am. Elijah! No interference!"

They win. Twenty-something to nothing. Good job, Baby. Sitting out here for hours in this cold was worth it.

I walk towards the field to congratulate my baby, but the coach stops me.

"Same thing applies on the field for games, Mrs. Brent. You can't come close to Lyric. You have no reason to be here."

"I'm just getting Elijah and leaving."

"He will meet you in the car, Mrs. Brent."

"Okay."

I walk away embarrassed. But I will not apologize for protecting my son. He meets me at the curb and waits for a cab with me.

"Elijah, I know that you want to go celebrate with your teammates. But not tonight. I need you focused on the bigger game—life. Steer clear of these hoes. And that's what Lyric is. Okay?"

"Yes, Ma'am," he answers. "And I want you to stop drinking. It's not going to fix what you are trying to ignore. I am—"

"Stay in a child's place!" I scream.

Eyes are all on me. People are whispering to each other. Some are laughing. Some are sad for me. What matters most is that I embarrassed Elijah. I apologize to him, he accepts, and we quietly ride home in a cab.

interVENTion

Chapter 4

7 Year old Aniyah

"Mommy! Mommy! Buy me that one! I want that one!"

"Aniyah, I already picked you out a doll. You're not getting two dolls. Let's go!"

"I don't want two dolls. I want this one. Put the one that you picked out back."

"What's wrong with the one I picked out? Why is the one you picked better than the one I picked?" she asked me.

"This doll looks like me! The one you picked doesn't look like me. At all. This doll is a Black boy. You picked out a White boy doll."

"Aniyah, stop being racist!"

"I'm not being racist. I don't even know what that means," I stated, confused. "I just want to play with a doll who looks like me."

"This doll that I picked out looks like you, Aniyah."

"No, it doesn't, Mommy. She looks like you. You are White. I'm not."

"You are my child, and I am White. That means you have White blood in you!"

"But I'm Black."

inter~~Ver~~VENT~~ion~~

"You are Black *and* White. You can't ignore one half of who you are. You have to acknowledge the entire picture, Aniyah."

"I don't ignore that I'm half White, Mommy. I just want a doll who looks like me."

"You're going to play with this doll!" she screamed at me.

"You don't play with brown dolls. Why do I have to play with White dolls?" I cried.

"I don't play with dolls at all because I am grown! You are a child! You are a child who is going to do what I say because I am grown, and I am your mother!"

"But you have dolls around the house to decorate the rooms, and they aren't brown. You have dolls that look like you. Why can't I have one doll that look like me? Just one?!" I continued to cry.

"No! The doll that I chose is perfect! There is no need for you to distinguish between these two dolls. There is no difference! Now, you apologize for carrying on like this!"

"If there's no difference, get me the brown one! I want the brown one! I don't want the White one! If I had a son, he would be brown, not White. It doesn't make sense for me to have a White doll!"

"Quit throwing a tantrum! You are being a silly spoiled brat! I am White, and I had a brown daughter and brown sons. You are brown, and you can have a White son. Apologize!"

"No, I can't!" I screamed. "Brown doesn't fade away like that. I can't have White children! It doesn't make sense that I have White dolls! I just want one brown doll. Just one. Who looks like me. Please, Mama," I begged her, crying, on my knees, holding on to her ankles.

"You don't need a doll who looks like you. I have a daughter who doesn't look like me, and I'm not throwing you back, am I?"

"You chose to have me. And I'm choosing to have a brown doll."

"No! Apologize for wanting me to put this doll back just so you can get another doll. You are ungrateful, selfish, and you think that that brown doll is better than the White doll. You think that brown is better! You don't see the beauty and perfection in the White doll because you are too focused on the Black doll. That Black doll is clouding your judgment and your view! Apologize for your behavior!"

At seven, I didn't understand the depth of that conversation. I didn't know why I felt so compelled to defend a *doll* who couldn't feel. There was something deep down inside that told me this spat with my mother wasn't really about an inanimate object: it was about the visible, tangible aspects of the object. For whatever reason, this doll being brown was causing division between my mom and me.

inter~~VEN~~Tion

     I didn't really comprehend that I was biracial. I didn't even know what biracial meant. My mind hadn't gone to those borders, yet. I didn't understand that I was Black girl with a White mom. I knew that, but those facts held no weight until that moment in the store. I didn't understand that even to my mama, my being Black was a problem.

     All I knew was that the doll looked like me. It was so rare to find a brown boy doll, but here he was. My twin! I was brown; he was brown. His hair was kinky; my hair would get kinky before my mama put chemicals in it to make it manageable for her. The doll's nose was wide; my nose was wide. His lips were thick; my lips were thick.

     I found a toy that I could identify with. What was wrong with that? Why didn't my mama want me to be able to relate to a brown doll? It was obvious to me: the doll is brown like me, so get the brown doll for me!

     All I could think was, "Why am I crying about a brown doll? Why does my mama want me to have a White doll so bad? What is wrong with brown? If there's something wrong with brown, then there's something wrong with me. Why do I have to apologize for identifying with a brown doll? Is something wrong with this doll? This doll looks like me. Is there something wrong with me?"

     My eyes opened that day to my skin color. My thinking was no longer shallow when it came to me being brown skinned and my mama being white skinned. It was blurry, but I could see that there was some kind of power struggle that came with the skin tones. I didn't know who had the power, who was greater, or who held the championship belt, but I knew *one* of them did—not both.

I began to look at myself differently that day. I began to not only notice my skin color but other peoples' skin color as well. My eyes were opened to the fact that I was Black, my mama was White, and she did not understand me. My White mama had no intentions of trying to understand me.

She felt that because she was White, she was right. She felt that because she was my White mother, she had every right to force her desires on me. She believed that because she was my White mother, she could downplay me in my own eyes and make me believe that there was nothing special about being Black. She wanted me to accept that White was right in every situation. She wanted me to choose White.

But I chose me. And I damn sure as hell didn't apologize for it.

I didn't know what "unapologetically Black" was, but that day I evolved into Her. That day, I didn't know that I would have to explain my Blackness the rest of my life. I didn't know that that would be a repeat conversation with thousands of people throughout my lifetime. I damn sure didn't know that my mama's and my relationship would never be the same after that day. My opened eyes caused a division between us that followed me into adulthood.

What I did know was that if my own mama didn't understand, other people didn't either. It was obvious that she didn't want to understand. How she felt was more important than how her daughter felt. How she perceived the situation carried greater weight than how her daughter would have to carry around the "burden" of being Black for the rest of her life. When she could have taken the time to nurture her daughter's Blackness, she instead was offended by it.

Mama's reaction said it all: brown is not welcomed here. I soon began to realize that we were not arguing about a doll; we were arguing about my realizing that I was Black. We were arguing about my being Black and proud. We were arguing about my being Black and loud. We were arguing about my finding nothing at all wrong with brown but everything wrong with White as it pertained to me.

I couldn't name one good thing about that White doll, and she couldn't stand it. I gawked over the beauty of brown, and she wasn't prepared for that. Maybe she thought that she could brainwash me into thinking and believing that I needed to be something that I wasn't. She so wanted to water down the power and beauty of brown that I was aware of.

But she was too late. I already loved myself. She couldn't get me to think that anything was wrong with me. At seven, she couldn't get me to have the thought that anything was better than brown.

My mama wanted the Black dick, but she didn't want the Black kids. She wanted the Black man, but she didn't want the problems that came with the Black man—Black kids. But I gave her hell in that store. I didn't walk out with the Black doll. But I walked out with more than I walked in with: self awareness.

She treated her daughter no differently than the rest of the world would treat me. She should have been my place of refuge, but she wasn't. What she did become that day was my biggest lesson: don't EVER expect to be liberated by my oppressor.

I went home after leaving the store and cried over that Black boy doll. I wanted him so badly that I envisioned him in my arms. I sang to him, rocked him to sleep, fed him, changed his diapers—all in my imagination.

I prayed for God to give me something that my mama couldn't take away—a Black son. Twenty three years later, God answered my prayers and gave me Elijah. He looked just like that doll. Just like that doll was perfect to me when I was seven years old, Elijah was undoubtedly perfect to me when I was thirty.

interVENTion

Chapter 5

Ocean

inter~~VENT~~ion

Yes! They showed up! They are really here to celebrate Elijah's birthday with him! I knew they would come to his birthday party. I told Elijah they would show up!

So many people have shown up that cars are overtaking the neighborhood. Elijah is a great kid. I'm not the only one who knows this. Elijah has to be so happy that people showed up! I told him that his birthday being so close to Christmas wouldn't stop people from coming this year. It's his sweet sixteen. No one with a heart would miss this.

I've spent all morning decorating and getting things in order for his birthday party. Montrel sent me to the store for last minute items. I was worried when I left because no one had shown up. But now that I'm back, the house is full of guests.

I open the door, and no one looks happy. I have a house full of people, and they all are looking solemnly at me. This is a party! Why so gloomy?

"Y'all. Where is the music? This is a party! What is the matter?" I ask, as I head for the stereo.

"Niyah, we need to talk," Montrel tells me, as he stops my hand from turning on the stereo.

"Trel, not now. Not ever."

"Now, Aniyah," some unknown White woman tells me.

"And who are you?" I ask.

inter~~ion~~**VENT**~~ion~~

"I am Dr. Angelique White. Everyone here loves you. They are here because they love you. And because they love you, they have asked me to do an intervention with you."

"Intervention?! I don't need no got damn—"

"Yes, you do, Aniyah," LaTrice says to me.

"And who invited you here?! You know you ain't welcomed here in my home! Get out!"

"I invited her here, Aniyah. I did. She could have called the police on you and had you committed for harassing her daughter all the time, but she didn't. Trice is not the enemy. Her daughter is not the enemy. You are your own enemy," Montrel tells me.

"*You* are my enemy, Montrel!"

"I am not your enemy! Aniyah, You are throwing a birthday party for our son who has been dead for ten years! You need help!

"Elijah is dead! He has been dead for ten years! He's going to be dead for ten years times ten years times one hundred years times infinity years! He is not here! Get some help, Aniyah! Elijah ain't here, and he ain't coming back!"

"How can you say that?" I ask Montrel, tears trickling down. "How can you so nonchalantly say that?"

"Because it's the truth," he answers calmly.

"So everyone here thinks I'm crazy?" I ask the room.

"No. We think you need help," my mom answers. "Any mama in your situation would need help. I have buried three children. I know the unbearable pain. I went and saw someone so that I could get help, Baby. You should, too."

"Aniyah, you were at his funeral. You were there when they lowered his casket into the ground. You have to know that Elijah is no longer here," Trice says to me. "Don't you?"

I shake my head. I'm not dealing with this today. I'm not hearing any of this. All of these people have teamed up on me. This is an unfair fight. I have nothing to prove to these people who "love me". If they love me, I sure hate to see how they treat people whom they hate. As I begin to walk upstairs to apologize to Elijah for how his party has turned out, someone grabs my hand.

"Do you remember me?" her soft, tender, whimpering voice asks.

I pause and stare into her core. My beautiful girl. My sweet, sweet baby girl. Of course I remember her. She is my daughter, my first born. I carried her for thirty-nine weeks and six days. Nineteen hours of labor. I breastfed her for three years until Elijah was born. How could I ever forget her? Impossible.

"Yes, Ocean. Hey, Sweetie. How are you?"

"I'm not fine, Mama. I want to live here, in the house with you and Trel. I always have wanted to live with you instead of Daddy. But you are so consumed with Elijah that you haven't acknowledged me since he died. I miss you so much. I want you to be better."

"Mrs. Brent, can you please come sit down?" Dr. White asks me.

I scan the room, and hurt and anguish is in everyone's eyes. Just to appease everyone, I decide to sit down.

"Mrs. Brent, I don't mean to sound abrupt or rude, but these are the facts: if you don't comply with me, you will be committed to a psychiatric facility. Do you understand that? These are the cards that you are playing with."

"I understand," I answer.

"Okay. Do you know that Elijah Thomas Brent is deceased?"

My stomach turns and twists into a knot. She doesn't know me like that to handle me like this! Who does she think she is?!

"What my son may or may not be is none of your concern."

"I agree. But *you* are my concern. All you have to do is answer the question."

"Yes," I huff.

"Yes, what?" she asks me

"I'm answering your question, Angelique, whom I didn't invite into my home."

"Can you say that you know that your son is dead?"

"That you know that your son is dead," I repeat.

"Okay, Mrs. Brent. I told you the cards that you were being dealt, and this is how you want to play. You will be admitted to a psychiatric facility tonight."

"Whoa, Dr. White. Hold on," Montrel tells her. "Niyah, Baby. This ain't what I want. I don't want you to go. I don't want you admitted anywhere."

"Who initiated this 'intervention'?" I ask him.

"I did because I love you and miss you."

"Well, miss me some more. I'm leaving. I'm going to this facility that you also initiated."

"No, Aniyah. All you have to say is, 'I know Elijah is dead.' Just say that. Let's start there," he begs me.

I take deep breaths to say it. I clear my throat to say it. I scan the room to prove these bitches wrong. But I can't prove them wrong. I can't say it. Not in a complete sentence like that.

"I know that—," I take another deep breath. "I am well aware—." I feel myself begin to go into a panic attack.

"Aniyah, it's okay," LaTrice runs to me and holds me. "You are okay. We are all here because we want to help you through this. Just breathe, Niyah."

She teaches me how to breathe correctly.

"I need to go to that facility," I admit. "I'll go. Just tell me what I need to do."

"No," Trel begs me. "Baby, no. Let's work on it here. Together."

"Mr. Brent. It's best if she goes. She should have been gone. It's okay."

"Well, what are they going to do with her? Dope her up so bad that she can't talk?"

"No. But she will be medicated. The lowest effective dose there is. She needs help. And medication is the start."

"She has meds in the cabinet upstairs. I can just give them to her every day."

"If she hasn't been taking them up to this point, there's a good chance that she still won't."

"I can sneak it in her food. Her drinks. Something. Please don't take my wife."

"You knew the possibility when we arranged this."

"I didn't think she would need it."

"She does, Mr. Brent."

They talk over me as if I'm not here. As if I can't hear. As if I'm a child who can't speak for herself or make her own decisions.

"I'm ready to go," I finally say.

Montrel grabs my hips, squeezes, lays his head on my shoulder, and says, "Baby, just say it."

"It's not that easy," I admit. "I would if I could."

Chapter 6

Weapons of Mass Destruction

"Do you have weapons of any sort?" the admissions person asks me.

"No."

They have me to strip. They take my shoelaces out of my shoes, tear my zipper off of my jacket, take the elastic out of my pants, and even search my maxi pads for hidden drugs.

"I'm in denial, not a suicidal or homicidal crack head," I say.

"Policy, Ma'am," she says.

After weighing and answering an immeasurable amount of questions, a tech walks me to my cold, punishing room. I do my best to "settle in", but it is not home. It feels like prison. Never mind. People in prison have more freedom than this.

"Here. Take these."

"What is this, and who are you?" I ask her.

"I'm your nurse until ten tonight. This is Librium. It's going to help you with alcohol withdrawals."

"Huh?"

"You're an alcoholic. You can't drink in here. Take this pill so that you don't go through terrible withdrawals."

"Oh, hell naw," I express, as I begin gathering my belongings.

I came here to deal with Elijah. Not to stop drinking. I'm not even an alcoholic. I could stop at any time if I wanted to. *IF* I wanted to. I don't want to stop; therefore, I'm not going to.

Drinking numbs the pain. Drinking takes away the sting. I don't feel the agony when alcohol is in my system. I agreed to an intervention about my son. Not an intervention about my drinking.

"Mrs. Brent. Are you leaving?"

"Yes, Nurse I-Don't-Know-What-Your-Name-Is."

"My name is Treasure. Why are you leaving? You have a problem with Librium? You want another way to treat alcohol withdrawal? You want no treatment for withdrawal and shake to death? What do you want?"

"I want to drink! Dr. White said nothing about me not being able to drink in here."

"Mrs. Brent, I'm sorry that she didn't tell you everything. But you are in a treatment facility. You will get treated for everything."

"I didn't ask for that. I didn't even ask for a fucking intervention, but I'm here! I did y'all a favor. Do me a favor. Let me drink."

"Mrs. Brent, getting help is doing yourself a favor. My check looks the same whether you stay or leave."

"Goodbye."

I stomp to the front door, and I can hear my daughter's voice in my head. "I miss you, Mommy. I want you better." I am already here. Being here is half the battle. If I am here, I might as well stay. And if I will stay, I might as well try. If I try, I might as well get better. If I don't like it after giving it a try, I can leave.

"Give me the pills," I tell Nurse Treasure, standing in front of her at the nurses' station.

"I threw them away."

"Those were the only ones in this building?" I ask.

She smirks at me and hands me the four pills. "That is one hundred milligrams. Each pill is twenty-five milligrams. You will be tapered down to no pills over the course of six days. I'm not saying that you won't have the desire or urge to drink. I'm not even saying that you won't have withdrawals. I'm just saying you won't have *bad,* life threatening withdrawals."

This is for my daughter Ocean I say to myself and swallow the pills.

****

inter~~ion~~VENT~~ion~~

"Mrs. Brent, please stop coming up to this nurses station."

"Miss Treasure," I pant. "All I'm asking you to do is just give me about two ounces of *any* kind of alcohol, and I will leave you alone."

"No, Ma'am. You have been asking me that for the last three nights that you have been here. No!"

"Okay. You don't have to give it to me. Just let me go out and get it. I promise you that I will come right back."

She stares at me and says nothing.

"What you like? I have a closet full of Michael Kors purses that I have never worn. You want a pair of Louboutins? My husband can afford anything you want. *Anything.* Just say it. I'll get it for you. You want your mortgage paid this month? Car windows tented out? What?"

She continues to silently stare at me.

"There has to be *something* that you want. You can't possibly have everything that you want. You are lacking somewhere. I know. Just name your price."

"Do you have a death wish, Mrs. Brent?" she asks me.

"No. I just want a taste of alcohol to take the edge off. Is that a crime? I'm grown! I'm old enough to drink. Let me drink. This is America! I have rights!" I scream, as I slam my hand down on her desk.

"You are absolutely correct," she calmly states. "You have the right to die. In the free country of America, you have the right to drink yourself to the grave because this free country don't care about you as long as you pay your way until you die. You are an adult who has the right to kill herself with alcohol.

"You have Librium and other anti-psychotic meds in your system that do not mix well with alcohol at all. If you drink *any* kind of alcohol, you *will* die. Is that what you want? You want to die, Mrs. Brent? Did you come here to kill yourself? Or did you come here to restore the relationship between you and your daughter? Because you can't do both. You can't make it right with her from the grave."

This bitch. What does she know about me and my daughter? How dare she go there? She is out of line. She is cruel. She is heartless. She is cold.

She is right.

I drag myself back to my room, continuing my detox of the deadliest weapon known to man: alcohol.

interVENTion

Chapter 7

Healing isn't a Fraction

inter~~ven~~VENT~~ion~~

"Welcome, Mrs. Brent. I am one of the therapists here Mr. Brite. This is our group therapy. I understand that you have been here for five days, but you have been going through withdrawals, so you haven't been able to attend these classes.

"On Wednesdays, it's a free flow conversation. Not as structured as Mondays, Tuesdays, and Fridays. On Thursdays and the weekends, there is no group. You are free to introduce yourself, start a conversation, whatever."

"Hello. I am Aniyah, and I am pissed that y'all won't let me drink."

"Amen, Sista!" a patient agrees.

"I agreed to come here to get healed from my son. Not to stop drinking. Dr. White left that part of the story out when she abducted me from my home."

"Mrs. Brent, I am sorry for the surprise. But we believe that you can't be healed if you are still holding on to what makes you sick. You can't be healed from your son's death if you still have Alcoholism Disease. Your mind won't heal when your spirit is always intoxicated. Your spirit can't heal if your mind is chemically altered.

"Healing means the *entire* body. We aren't going to neglect any sick part of you. You can't cherry pick your healings. If any part of you is sick, all of you is sick.

"Sickness is a cancer. If there is any part of you that is well, the sickness will spread until it eats away the healthy part of you, and all of you will become sick. The real question is why do you want to drink?"

"To numb the pain of my son."

"How about you allow that pain to resonate so that the healing process can begin?"

"That's the dumbest shit I've ever heard," I answer.

"Alcohol don't heal shit, Mrs. Brent," Mr. Brite begins. "Alcohol may numb the pain, but it doesn't cure it. It may make the pain more bearable temporarily, but it didn't erase the pain. Alcohol prolongs the healing process while it makes the situation worse. How about you allow us to help heal that pain so that you won't need the alcohol? It's a two for one deal. No pain, no alcohol needed."

"Well, the pain is here right now! I tried it y'all's way the last five days! This pain has deepened!"

"That's because you're finally sober, and you can finally feel."

I think about what he just said. I *am* finally sober. Sobriety brought pain with him.

Mr. Brite continues, "Your addiction didn't start when your son passed. You didn't lose mental

control because of your son. Your mental illness is the
result of an accumulation of pain after pain, incident
after incident that you have been trying to bury. Your
son's death is what took you over the edge. The straw
that broke the camel's back if you will.

"People don't end up in a facility like this
from *one* incident. People end up here because they
snapped. Your demons that you have not confronted
have eaten away at you until your mind, body, and
soul couldn't handle anything else. Demons don't go
away on their own. And they always bring their
friends. You have to confront your demons and make
peace with them. That's the only way to get rid of
them and start healing. When was the first time you
had a drink?"

"I was fifteen," I answer.

"What made you drink?" a patient asks me.

I dance around the question with answers that
take people in circles. It's no one's business, I don't
want to talk about it, and I won't talk about it.

"Tell us about your son. Elijah, right?" Mr.
Brite inquires.

"Yes," I exhale. If I can't do anything else, I
can talk about my baby boy. "He is an all around
great kid. His smile is contagious. His laugh makes
people laugh. He is never angry. He never throws a
temper tantrum. And he loves football. Oh, my God,

football is his life. He is so fast and so precise. No doubt, an athlete.

"He is on the little league team. He is their star player. Number four jersey. His nickname is Lightning because he is so fast. If you blink, you'll miss him. He wins every game. His team never ever loses. My Number Four does that."

I pause to tell the part of the story that never changes. No matter how many times I tell the story, it never changes. It always ends the same.

"One day during football practice, he was running, then he... stopped," I continue. "He just stands there, looks at me, and drops to the ground."

I take a deep breath to prepare myself to talk about him in the past tense.

"He was six years old. I ran onto that field. I don't even remember getting up out of the bleachers. He wasn't breathing at all. Some doctor who was at the game performed CPR on him, but there was no use. The CPR got his heart back to pumping and lungs back to working, but mentally, he was gone.

"He was declared brain- dead and a vegetable. They had him on all these machines, just pumping air into him. But he wasn't here on Earth anymore. I told them to turn the machines off. That was no way to live.

interVENTion

"The autopsy revealed that he was born with a heart defect that kills babies in their first year of life when gone untreated. Elijah kept going until he couldn't go no more. There were never any signs of this said heart condition. He never showed signs of anything being wrong.

"When I made the decision to take him off of life support, I wasn't mentally here. I was floating and just existing. Things had happened so fast that I didn't have time to process what was going on and what was happening. I didn't really swallow that my son had... you know. I just was going along with the process: medical decisions, funeral arrangements, burial policies. I just went with the flow.

"Then when things settled down and the visitors started lightening up, I had nothing but time. Time with myself. Time with quiet space. Time with time. And like a train railroading its way into my chest, I couldn't breathe. I literally couldn't catch my breath. The only thing that would cure that feeling was having my son back.

"Why did I take him off of life support? Even if he was a vegetable, I would still have him. I didn't care that he would have been a special needs child; I would still have him.

"To relieve the pain, I decided that he was alive, and Hennessey helped me to keep that belief. Me deciding that he was still here started off as something to just help me cope. I wasn't hurting anyone, so there was nothing wrong with it. I went to football games, acting like he was there, cheering him on. I missed days from work to go to his Field Days at school that he clearly wasn't at.

"I went to the youth's choir rehearsal at church every Tuesday night to hear him sing. Crazy thing is, my daughter was actually at those rehearsals, but I wasn't there for her. I didn't even realize that she was there.

"Somewhere along the lines, the lines got blurred. Reality subtly faded away, and my fantasies took over. I began hurting people through harassment and embarrassment. I hurt those who were the closest to me. I destroyed my marriage. And I've possibly forever destroyed the bond between my daughter and me. She faded away over the years because of my denial, neglect, and abandonment. My denial has severed ties that can never be mended again."

"Mrs. Brent, no one stopped you? Those closest to you? They were aware that you were rearranging your life for events that weren't even happening. They just let you? What about at those choir rehearsals when you were there for Elijah who was dead?" a patient asks me.

"In the beginning, people just let me be. It was like I said: as long as I wasn't hurting anyone. As long as I was still a functioning member of society. When I no longer was a functioning member of society, they started saying things here and there that I would quickly shut down.

"As far as my church members go, I am a member of a Black Baptist church. They believe in 'praying away the pain'. As long as I was in church, it didn't matter that I was losing my fucking mind. They just would pray for me, spiritually put me on the altar, tell me that joy comes in the morning, and go on about their days.

"That's the thing about Black people and religious people—they don't believe in getting mental help. They want to keep the mental health issues hush hush, look away, don't talk about it. If you see a therapist, you're crazy and don't have faith in God.

"My faith in God tells me that I need more than God; I need help. And I'm here to get it. The answer to my prayers is therapy. God sent therapy. And if I am crazy, so what? I'm in the right place— getting help. I now believe that it is okay for me to have Jesus *and* therapy.

"My church family knew that I'm an alcoholic who was saying that my son was the one drinking all the alcohol in the house, and they just prayed for me. They knew that I wasn't coping well, and they just prayed for me. They knew that I had never accepted my son's… you know… and you know what they did? Prayed for me. When I lost my business due to my alcoholism and denial, there they were, praying.

"But faith without works is dead. Praying and not-doing doesn't work. Praying and looking away doesn't work. Praying and sweeping it under the rug resolves nothing. Praying and ignoring is ineffective.

"My friends and family... they prayed for me. Overlooked the issue. Played along to some degrees. As long as I wasn't hurting anyone, they swept it under the rug. Then when I began to harass and be an embarrassment, 'Take your medicine, Niyah.'

"But I was far gone. Beyond medicinal help. Medicine alone would have helped in the beginning. Not now, though. I need more than medicine. I need an intervention. After ten years, my people got me what I needed. And I'm here. I just want to be better. I have to be better for my nineteen year old daughter if for no other reason."

"And if you accept all of our suggestions, you will be better. But I can promise you one thing: we are not going to discharge you if you can't say the words, 'my son is dead'. Not 'gone'. Not 'not here anymore'. But 'dead'," Mr. Brite tells me.

"Then I will definitely see y'all at the next session," I reply.

Chapter 8

Sins of the Father

"Niyah, I just want you healthy. Mentally, spiritually, emotionally. I want you back. But I want you to have you back most of all. Don't you miss you?" my husband asks me at my visitation.

"Yes, I do. That is why I'm here. I want to get back to me. I am doing everything I'm supposed to do. I take my meds. I exercise. I eat a well-balanced meal. I am not noncompliant at all. So, I'm not understanding why you are acting like I am being irrational or uncooperative."

Montrel sighs, "I don't know. I just don't know. I don't like this. You in here like... like..."

"Like I'm crazy."

He looks me in my eyes, and his pain is so deep. He would never use the word "crazy", but that is the word. His heaviness is so evident at my visitation that my chest is sinking in for him.

"You are not crazy. You are human. Baby, I am so sorry."

"What are you sorry for? You didn't kill him."

"I killed you. I left you to deal with that pain alone. I was hurting, too. I was hurting so fucking bad. I was mad. I wanted answers, and nobody could tell me shit! How the fuck my son went six years with a bad heart, and none of them doctors caught it?!

"I couldn't breathe, Aniyah. I went into the closets and cried all day long. I cried in the shower. I cried in the car. I cried at my desk at work. I cried at the bars. I cried in stores' parking lots. I cried in the deacons' office at church. I cried everywhere, except with you.

"I left you to hurt alone. To cry alone. I made you feel like you were by yourself in your pain, but you weren't. Everything you felt, I felt. We should have felt them together. You were brave enough to grieve, and I hated you for that.

"Whenever you would come to me, I wanted to be the masculine man. I didn't want to seem like a bitch. So, I was your shoulder. I tried to be your rock. I should have showed you that I was human, just like you. That I was crying, just like you.

"I made it seem as if you were crazy. Like you shouldn't have been feeling what you were feeling. I left you alone, Aniyah. Our marriage began failing because I left you alone. I wasn't there. We should have gone through this together. I am so sorry," Montrel cries.

"Trel, I forgive you, and I understand."

"I missed my little boy so much. So, when you first started saying what Elijah was doing, I didn't stop you because I didn't want to let him go, yet. It felt good to hear that my little boy won football player of the year. My son was crushing on a little girl. My son made a hundred on his math test.

"But you didn't stop, and the stories became bigger. You began harassing people, lying on people, ruining your friendships. You couldn't work because you had to take an imaginary person on trips and to camp. We lost so much money on make believe. It went too far. And I accept the blame for that as well. I should have stopped you from the beginning. I should have been a better husband all around.

"I am sorry. But I'm starting now. When you get out, I'm taking you to Paris like you've always wanted."

"I appreciate that. I really do. But I'm getting a job as soon as they release me. We are really in the hole financially because of me. I've already had my Paris. I'm going to start pulling my weight. It's all been on you for the last ten years. I'm done being the victim. We are a team. I'm ready to do my part."

He gently grabs my hands. "Do your part after Paris. The both of us can use the break."

"Ocean should come. I owe her so much. I have missed her entire childhood. Ballet recitals, t-ball games, graduations. I've missed them all. How can I make that up?"

"You can't. You just have to be there starting now. I discussed Paris with her. And she's not ready for a trip like that with you. She doesn't even want to come here and visit you. Don't take it personal."

"Tell her to come see me. Please."

"I have. But she's nineteen. She's grown. She makes her own decisions. I can't make her."

"I'm going to write her a letter. I'll have it ready when you come see me tomorrow."

"Okay. I love you with all that I have, Aniyah. We can and will make it through this."

"Yes, we will."

"Baby, can you just say out loud that Elijah is dead so that they can start the discharge process on you? I want you home. Now."

"No, Trel, I can't. And after I say it, they said I have to go see his... you know."

"His tombstone?" Trel asks me.

"Yes. I damn sure can't stomach that. So, I'm here for the long haul. They won't let me go home until I see it in person."

"Do you think God killed our son because of our sins?" Trel asks me.

"Yeah. I do."

Chapter 9

Montrel and Aniyah in the
Beginning

"Mrs. Lewis, I hate to cut our meeting short, but something important has come up at Headquarters. Can we meet again and discuss this further?"

"Yes, Mr. Brent, we can."

"I have one more question. Can I leave my car here for a few hours? You're not going to have it towed or anything, will you?"

"Yes, you can," I laughed. "I won't have it towed. I will be leaving in about four more hours. I can't promise the safety of your car after that. When I leave, security leaves."

"Thank you, Mrs. Lewis."

Montrel Brent ran out the building. He was in such a rush that he didn't even take the elevator; he took the stairs. I was no fool. I was his accountant, and I knew where his money came from. It was never my place to ask him any questions or confront him about anything. As long as he paid me like he was supposed to, I had no problems with him. He was pleasant, friendly, courteous, and respectful. That is all that mattered.

Four hours passed, and he hadn't returned. I wasn't going to wait on him, either. I sent the security guard home, and I began locking up the place. Right before I put the security code in, I heard knocks on the door. It was Montrel.

Teasing him, I stood in front of the door, shaking my head.

"Mrs. Lewis. Don't do me like that," he laughed.

"Closed!" I yelled.

"I know. But I left my keys on your desk."

"I know," I shrugged.

"Mrs. Lewis! You are right in the building! Just go get the keys, bring them to me, and I will leave you alone."

"I've already clocked out."

"You own the place! Come on, please."

I opened the door to let him in.

"You better be glad I'm in a good mood today."

"I'm ever so grateful."

He got on the elevator with me.

"Where you from, Mrs. Lewis?"

"Decatur where it's greater."

"I figured that," he smirked.

"What is that supposed to mean?"

We walked off the elevator to my desk. I handed him his keys that I had placed in my locked drawer.

"You know how to see and not see. Hear and not hear. You don't ask no questions, but you know what's up," he answered.

"I know that you pay me on time, every time."

"Right," he smiled at me.

"And I know that if that Rolls Royce was in front of my building when I came back in the morning, it was going to be mine. Finders, keepers."

"You want it? I'll give it to you. Or if you want your own, I'll buy it for you. As a thank you gift for all you've done."

"My clients usually buy me flowers, chocolate covered fruits, twenty-five dollar gift cards. A Rolls Royce is—"

"When did I become just a client? I haven't been just a client in a while."

My insides began to tremble from nervousness. He was right. In my mind, we had made love a million times, and he was so good at it. Whenever he walked in the room, I would say to myself, "There's my boo. Zaddy. My side piece. My future baby step-daddy."

inter~~VENT~~ion

The way he would look at me made me cream. The way he would talk to me made me dance inside as if I was a school girl. The way he breathed… made me feel privileged to breathe the same air as he.

Him… Gotdamned Him.

But we'd never done anything. Only in our fantasies. Our eyes told each other our creamiest thoughts every time we met.

"Mr. Brent, I don't know what you mean."

He grabbed the picture of me, my husband, and my daughter Ocean off of my desk.

"Beautiful family, Aniyah."

He had never called me by my first name before. The way he said it… with such passion… such consideration to pronounce it correctly…with his Latin accent… gotdamn.

"Thank you. Where are you from?" I asked him.

"Atlanta. But both of my parents are from Puerto Rico, so my accent is strong. Neither one of them speak English. Even though my dad is Black, he was born there to a military dad, and he never really picked up on English. So, my dad is an African Puerto Rican. Dark skin. Wide nose. Kinky hair. His entire family is African American, and he can't speak English. The military moved them here before I was born. My mom is full blooded Puerto Rican."

inter~~VENT~~ion

"You ever been to Puerto Rico?" I asked him.

I don't know at what point we both sat down, but we were sitting, smiling, joking, laughing, and enjoying conversation with each other.

"I didn't go until I was nineteen. Now, I go damn near every month. It's a beautiful place. Shit they don't show on TV. My parents, wife, and son are the only family I have here. So, I always go to Puerto Rico."

"Estar con tus primos, tias, tios, y abuelos?"

"So you been holding out on me. You speak my language in every way," he sensually spoke.

"Answer the question."

"Yes. I go to be with my cousins, aunts, uncles, and grandparents."

"Well, I will see you next time. Let me walk you out."

He grabbed me by my waist. "I want you."

It wasn't a question, option, or a suggestion. Not for my loins. It was a statement that required action. I had to do it. I had done it a million times in my mind; what was one time in reality?

I pushed everything off my desk onto the floor. Jumping on top of the desk, I pulled my panties off from underneath my skirt. I was reaching for his belt when he grabbed my hands, stopping me.

interVENTion

"I don't want you like *that*," he told me.

My pride was crushed. I had no way to play it off. I was so embarrassed. Sitting on top of my desk, juice box exposed, intentions unquestionable.

"I am so sorry, Mr. Brent. I—"

He picked me up and placed me in my chair. He got on his knees between my legs and looked me in my eyes.

"*This* is how I want you."

My body melted into his mouth, and I watched him drown.

interVENTion

Chapter 10

Cum-Passion

"Hi, Mrs. Lewis. Come on in."

"Thank you, Mrs. Brent. It's nice to finally meet you."

"You, too."

"Hi, Mr. Brent."

"Hello, Mrs. Lewis. We can go to my office."

"Okay," I agreed.

"Mrs. Lewis, thank you for meeting us at our home. Sometimes, my husband's… *business* calls unexpectedly, and he has to answer. So, thank you for understanding that and coming here to finish his paperwork."

"Oh, yes, Ma'am. No problem. I need to get away from my toddler," I laughed.

Trel walked me through his home to his office. We walked through an all white room with nothing in it, except a mirror on the wall and a chair—a gold throne. I was mesmerized by its elegance and cut. The wood was obviously hand carved. Special attention was paid to every detail. The high back, strong arms, bowed legs all enticed me. I found myself tracing the outline with my left index finger.

"You like this chair, Mrs. Lewis?" Trel asked me, breaking me out of my daze.

"Yes," I answered, embarrassed. "I do. It is gorgeous."

"Mrs. Lewis, you have done something that no one has ever done: you *touched* his sanctuary."

"I am so sorry!" I exclaimed.

He smirked at me and said nothing.

"Mrs. Lewis," his wife began, "this room is off limits to everyone except him. I can't believe he brought you through here. This room is called Passion because he comes in here and does what he is so passionate about: nothing. He sits right here and does nothing."

"My life is so busy, crazy, hectic, out of my control that I love being able to just do nothing. This room is my shrine. And my chair is my sanctuary."

"I am really sorry for defiling it. I—"

"It's okay. My office is this way."

He led us to his office. I took all the papers out and laid them on the table. His wife handed me a cold bottle of water.

"Thank you, Mrs. Brent," I thanked her.

"You can call me Lavender."

"That's a beautiful name."

"Thank you. My mom loved purple, so she named all of us something purple. Four girls and one boy. My sisters' names are Periwinkle, Violet, and Amethyst."

"Tell her your brother's name," Trel snickered.

"Boysenberry."

I literally spat my water out from laughing. "I am so sorry. I didn't mean to spit," I laughed. "That's not his name. No, it's not. Stop playing."

"My mama said she knew it was meant to be his name because she loves purple, and the first words are 'Boy'. If the first words are 'Boy', then surely she was meant to name her son that."

"I am speechless, Lavender."

"We all *still* are."

"You know, people talk about me because I named my daughter Ocean. But Boysenberry definitely beats Ocean."

"Ocean is beautiful. I think of peace when I think of the ocean."

"That's exactly why I named her that. I am a true beach bum. Before I had her, I was at my happiest with my feet in the water with sand between my toes. The ocean always brought me peace and calmed the storms of my mind.

"My labor was tumultuous. I thought I was going to lose my mind and die. Then they put her in my arms, and all that anxiety and fear that I felt vanished. She became my ocean—my serenity."

"That is beautiful, Mrs. Lewis."

"Aniyah. Call me Aniyah. Or Niyah."

"Okay. Well, you guys do this every month without me. Numbers aren't my language. I'm going to get our son ready for bed. Nice meeting you again, Aniyah."

"You, too, Lavender."

She left out of the room, and Trel and I handled his business. We never spoke about what happened between us the day before. We both knew that we had taken it too far. Our eyes told each other that. We were back to business as before.

When we finished, he walked me to the door. I could hear his wife and son upstairs. We walked through Passion again, and it took everything in me to not touch *his sanctuary*.

"Why do you look at my chair like that?" he asked me.

"No reason."

"You're lying."

Nervously laughing, I answered, "I would love one."

"Why?"

I looked him in his eyes and said, "Because I want to get head in it and feel like a king."

"Then have a seat, Your Highness."

He took my briefcase out of my hand and placed it wherever. I sat down as commanded. He squatted between my legs and made me feel the passion that he felt in his room.

His hands explored my continents. I gripped my crown as he clutched my pearls. His beard grazed my inner thighs. He placed his index and middle fingers in my mouth as he ate the king's platter. I sucked his two fingers like I was trying to get the last drop of a strawberry malt. He groaned; I moaned. He gripped; I grabbed.

"Sit on my face," he roared.

"Huh?" I insecurely asked.

"Sientate en mi cara," he repeated in Spanish, lifting me up off the throne, guiding my hips, placing me on top of his chin.

"Fuck my face," he growled.

"I don't know how," I admitted.

He moved my hips as he moved his tongue. My body adjusted, quivering, and it took over. My frame found a rhythm and danced on the floor of his face. As I grinded and slow wound, he placed his pinky in my secret anal entrance. That was new for me, and I didn't want him to stop. Ever. I don't know what universe he took me to, but there was plenty of water there.

He lifted my two hundred twenty two pounds of flesh up, placing me on his throne.

"Reign," he breathed into me.

And my reign rained everywhere. I reigned in his mouth, hair, eyelashes, nose. It rolled into his ears, down the sides of his neck. When I returned to Earth, I heard his wife and son upstairs. My husband flashed across my mind.

"Oh, my God! What are we doing?! Oh, my God! We are at your house! Your wife and son are upstairs! I have a husband!" I frantically whispered, as I fixed my clothes, looking for my briefcase. "We have lost our minds!"

I marched to the exit door of Passion, managed to get it slightly open, and his hand went above me, closing it. I looked up at his hand on the door, and there was a condom in between his index and middle fingers. I dropped my briefcase, slid my panties off, and bent over. He entered my world, and I was never the same.

interVENTion

Chapter 11

Idioma

"Mrs. Lewis," my secretary called into my office. "Your two o'clock is here."

"Okay. Send them in."

Trel walked in. "You haven't been answering my texts or calling me back. I was starting to get worried."

He sat down in front of my desk in the chair for customers. I was purposely avoiding him. I had nothing to say. I was embarrassed, upset, shocked— every emotion that there was to feel.

"I have a husband to worry about me. You don't get paid to do his job. And I don't need you filling in."

"His job? Ha! It was obvious you've never rode a man's face. You've never been picked up. You've never had your booty played with. Sounds like to me you *do* need somebody to do his job. And the way you pay—"

"Is there anything I can do for you, Mr. Brent?"

"Did I do something to you?!"

He was sincere in his question. I honestly had no answer.

"No. You didn't."

"Then, what's the problem?"

interVENTion

"We have to stop, Trel. That's the problem."

"We've already started, Aniyah. We can't take it back. Might as well keep going."

"I can't. Because I want to be your only one. It's obvious I'm not even one of two."

"What does that supposed to mean?"

"You had a condom, and you're married! You are out here fucking around."

"You weren't worried that I had a condom when you were throwing that ass back at me. You shole wasn't worried about the condom or other women when you took the condom off and swallowed my kids. So why the fuck you bringing it up now?"

"So, I'm not the only outside woman. Okay," my voice drifted away.

He grabbed my hand. "Aniyah, you are. I have never cheated on my wife. We use condoms for birth control because she can't take the pill. Honestly, there's only you. I don't even fuck my wife 'cause I'm trying to be faithful to my side chick—you. I gotta have you, Aniyah. I will risk it all for you. Just tell me to leave her, and I will. You leave Lenny, and—"

"Trel! You have lost your mind!"

"I know that you feel this. This connection ain't in my head. I know good and damn well that we are vibing."

"Vibing don't mean divorce and tear apart our families! You have a son. I have a daughter."

"Have you ever heard of blended families?"

"Am I even your type, Montrel? Your wife— she is your type. She speaks your language. She—"

"Just because she's Puerto Rican doesn't mean she's my type. And you speak my language—Spanish *and* Street."

"But she's one of you. I can't—"

"*You are me*. And I'm Black, too, remember?"

I honestly had forgotten that he was half Black. He was so light skinned with jet black silky hair and a Spanish accent that it was hard to see anything but Puerto Rican in him.

"And Blacks and Browns are all the same, Mama," he continued. "No disrespect to the struggle of your people. But I don't get respect or love from the White man, either. No company is jumping to give me a loan, either. I can't get a cab in New York, either. *We* are the same, Ma."

"I'm so different from your wife."

"Which is why I'm here and not wherever she is. That is the point. You aren't her. She ain't you. I want you. You understand the business, and you get me."

"She seemed like she understands pretty well to me."

"She understands that I provide. You understand that I breathe this shit."

interVENTion

Chapter 12

Montrel and Aniyah Now

"We were both married. We both had families. I had my daughter. You had your son. We both caused chaos in our homes. We had to be crazy to think that we weren't going to have to pay for what we did," I tell Montrel at my visitation.

"But we got married. We tried to make it right, Niyah. I tried to make it right. I even stopped selling drugs and got a real job. I got off these streets before he was born. I ain't did nothing shady since you were pregnant. And we got married!"

"But the sin had already been committed. We still had to pay the price for it."

"Please tell me we are done paying. I can't take no more."

"I don't know," I tearfully tell him.

"Time's up," the charge nurse announces to everyone.

"Aniyah. I don't want you to take this the wrong way, but I regret nothing. I don't regret you. Whatever had to happen as a consequence of us being together just had to happen. I want you. I love you. There's no way I can live without you.

"We going to get through it together this time, okay? Don't check out on me. Don't block me. And I won't act like I'm blind to your pain. We are going to do it right this time. I promise."

"Okay."

interVENTion

"I'm serious, Baby. We are going to cry together. Yell together. Go visit the gravesite together. We are going to get through this. I love you, dammit. I ain't going nowhere. And you ain't, either. It's us versus the world. You got me?"

"I sure do, Babe."

interVENTion

Chapter 13

Sixteen Years Ago

"Lenny, we have to talk," I told my husband.

"Yes, Babe? What's up? And I been meaning to tell you that you put yo' foot in them chicken and dumplings last night."

I stared at him silently. My heart was pounding in my throat. Generally, he was a good guy. Really. Just not good for me. I had known it before we got married. I knew it before we dated. I knew it when we were just friends. But I married him anyway thinking that the feeling would past. I made myself believe that the things that bothered me wouldn't bother me any more with time. I was wrong. If anything, they bothered me even more the older that I got.

"I want a divorce, Leonard," I blurted out.

"Aniyah, you always say that, but you never mean it. You do not want a divorce."

"Leonard, yes, I do. I have meant it every time. I don't want you. Period. The end. You are a nice guy. You're sweet. You're kind. You're gentle. You're just not for me."

"Yes, I am, Babe. Don't say that."

"You're not! You never have been!"

"Aniyah. You don't mean this."

"Lenny! Listen! **I DON'T WANT YOU! AT ALL! I NEVER HAVE! I NEVER WILL!**"

"I think you just need to nap. You've had a long day."

"This is part of the reason why I don't want you, Leonard! You're soft. Weak. Pathetic. Bitch ass nigga! I don't want you, and you're whining about it. Man up! I don't want no whimpering pussy bitch nigga! And that's what you are!

"You ain't did nothing but get fatter. Your dick done got shorter. It either won't get hard or won't stay hard. I'm sick of feeling your stomach rubbing my clit. If you trying to hit it from the back, you sit your stomach on my back, and I fucking cringe every time! How you can only fuck for four seconds before nutting with a soft dick, I don't know! But I'm sick of you!

"I'm sick of not being pleased. I'm sick of having to fantasize about somebody else while you rub me. I turn my head when you try to kiss me because I don't feel that level of intimacy with you.

"You are somebody I split the bills with. You are that man who takes the trashcan to the curb every Wednesday. You that nigga who picks up our daughter from piano practice. But you are not my *It*.

"I shriek inside when I think of being your wife. I want to be free of you and from you. You drain me. You make me tired. Your weakness wears me out.

"If I'm going to have to be the man of this house, what the hell are you here for? If I have to speak up every time somebody takes advantage of you, what the hell you got a dick for? If you can't handle business without stuttering, why am I in a skirt?!

"You can't fucking be a man! I'm sick of forgiving you for that! We are done! I'm ready to be a woman. I want to feel like a woman. I want to be a woman."

"Niyah, I can work on it."

"You've supposedly been working on it for over a decade. All you've done is gotten worse. You are selfish. You want me to sit around and be miserable and drained with you while you get worse. You want to be fat and happy while I'm horny and miserable. That is not fair to me. That's an evil plot you have going."

"It's not a plot, Niyah. I'm just... depressed all the time."

"And that's another thing. You know you're depressed, and you're doing nothing about it. Your depression depresses me! We can't have a good time because you're too busy worried about shit that you can't control. You see me having a good time, and you will find a way to slurp the fun out of me. If you find yourself having a good time, you're going to make sure you dead that real quick.

inter<u>VENT</u>~~ion~~

"I am still young! Being with you has aged me at the speed of light. You have taken away my youth and my love for life. You have left me as an empty, hollow shell. You have taken it all. You have drained me. I can't do this anymore. I. Just. Can't. I will not lose me to keep you."

"Let's go to counseling. I been telling you that ever since we got married. A therapist will help us."

"I'm pregnant."

"How? We use condoms every time. And I pull out with the condom on because I know how much you don't want to get pregnant."

I allowed my silence to answer his question. I saw his soul crumble through his iris. He rose up out of his seat, stood over me, grabbed my face, and said, "Say that again. I didn't hear you right."

If I ever doubted his manliness, it wasn't then. I slowly backed away from his grip and stated, "I am pregnant. And the baby is not yours."

"What the fuck you mean?! I'm your husband! How the hell am I not your baby's father?! I know you lying. You fucking with me." He began to laugh evilly. "Yea. You fucking with me."

I stood there, saying nothing. I allowed my tears to finish the conversation. He heard what they were saying loud and clear.

"That's what I get for fucking with yo' half breed ass!" he yelled at me.

"What's that supposed to mean?"

"Your mama White, and it's obvious by the way you act that you got White people blood in you. You tainted. Evil. Capable of doing this foul shit! I don't put nothing past you. You liable to do anythang. I was a fool to think that I could trust you. You Black, but you ain't one of us. That's been clear for a while."

"So now you're questioning my Blackness?"

"Anything you know about being Black, you learned from me. You didn't know real Black history until you got with me. All this stuff that you are so passionate about— rebuilding Black Wall Street, integration versus desegregation, building schools for our own children—all me.

"You had a sheltered childhood, being able to hide behind your *White* mama. Living in a house on a hill with butlers, maids, and shit. You never had to deal with *real* Black people's problems. Any heat that remotely came your way immediately cooled down when it got to your mama. You didn't start being Black until you were eighteen, living by yourself, away from your mama's White privilege. When you couldn't be protected by your mama's skin anymore, all of a sudden, you were *Black* Black.

"You and your brothers had the light brown skin with the good, curly hair. You don't know what it is to be a NIGGER! That's why you can't respect the grind, hustle, or effort that I have put forth for this family.

"I work three jobs, three different shifts just to make sure you and Ocean need nothing. I go on lunch break from one job to clock in on another job. I haven't slept in years. I haven't seen my own mama in months because I'm making sure that y'all want for nothing. I haven't been out with my boys, ain't seen no movie, ain't played nothing on the Playstation—nothing! Because I'm doing what I got to to make sure that you and our child have shit you never even dreamed of.

"Your company has more bills than it has clients, so I took it upon myself to work myself to death so that your failing business can stay afloat and you can keep on doing what you love. And you complaining that I have gained weight and can't get it up every time.

"I bet if I quit two of these damn jobs and actually get some sleep, I will lose weight and get it up! If I quit some jobs and let your business die and not be able to afford name brands for you and our daughter, I will have so much time to be able to dedicate to my health and be able to lose weight and get it up.

"But let me guess: you still won't want me then, either, will you? You don't have honor, admiration, or respect for a Black man trying his fucking best just like your mama didn't! My best ain't good enough for your privileged ass! It never has been. You don't live by the Black code like real Black people do.

"And I may not be the strongest man, but, dammit, do I get credit for trying? I may not handle business the best, but do you at least see that I *tried* to handle business? And it ain't that I don't speak up for myself. Everythang ain't gotta be a fucking war every time somebody gets out of line with me. If a fool and a wise person are arguing, which one is who? But you don't understand that because you always have to find fault with me.

"I was a fucking fool to give you my last name. I can't believe I laid down with your half and half ass! Whoever he is, he can have you. He can find out first hand for his damn self that you ain't shit! You don't respect a man as a man, and he will find that out.

"Being with you hasn't been a walk in the park, either, Aniyah, but because I respect our vows, I put my chin up and took all the blows. But that's the code I live by. You and your people have a different set of rules for your lives.

"Ain't no questioning your Blackness. I got all the answers. You your mama's child. Good bye."

"You right. I ain't no *real Black* woman because no Black woman in her right mind would have put up with this shit! Limp dick, weak, can't stand up to nobody, can't handle business, let people talk to you and treat you any kind of way, let people say whatever they want to say to you about your wife! You're not a protector of us. You barely provide because we *still* split these bills fifty-fifty. You can't make a decision. You won't put a coat on when it's cold outside unless somebody tells you to. You are so right! I ain't one of y'all. A real sista woulda *been* left yo'ass!"

I walked out, slamming the door behind me. I had nothing with me, except my debit card and car keys. For the first time in my life for over a decade, "not having" didn't worry me because I was finally with a man who I knew would provide—Montrel. And provide Montrel did.

Montrel found out that I was lacking, and he rescued me. I could breathe again once I left Leonard. I never looked back. I never felt guilty. I had been putting up with his insufficiency for ten years. It was time for me to live for me. That weight was off of my chest. I could breathe again. I was happy again.

I had peace again.

Chapter 14

Lenny's And Niyah's Divorce

inter~~inter~~**VENT**~~ion~~

I signed the divorce papers first. Lenny signed them after me. Everything was there in black and white. I let him have it all: the cars, house, land. I agreed to change churches. I left all the furniture in the house. All I wanted was my business and my daughter. He knew better than to fight me for either one, so he didn't. We all walked away from the table amicably.

"Aniyah," he grabbed my hand in the court's hallway. "Wait."

"What, Leonard?"

"What do we do now?"

"What do you mean? The papers that you just signed said that you keep the house, cars—"

"No. I know the technicalities. I mean… what do I do with my day now? How am I supposed to sleep? Where do I go after work? Ever since I was thirteen, and we were just best friends, my life revolved around you.

"My day was based on whatever you wanted to do. I rushed home from work to see you and take you wherever. I woke up early for work to be out of your way for when you woke up for work. I slept with the TV on because you are afraid of the dark, even though I can never truly rest with lights on and noise going.

inter~~ter~~**VENT**~~ion~~

"I don't even know what season of sports it is right now because you don't like sports, and I watched movies with you instead of catching the Lakers. I always made sure to keep the bananas up high on the shelf because you're allergic to them, and I knew that with them being up high, there was no risk of your short self touching them by accident.

"I park extremely close to the wall of the garage in my car to give you room to get out of your car. I haven't drunk a real soda since I was in college because all you drink is diet sodas because you are always worried about your weight. Every fucking thing in the house is turquoise because that's your favorite color, and I just wanted you to be happy.

"When I go to Waffle House, I'm going to think about how we went there every Saturday—rain, hail, sleet, snow, or sun. When I go to Wal-Mart, I'm going to remember how you always go in on the non-food side to give yourself time to warm up before you go to the groceries side.

"If I flick through the channels, I'm going to hear you screaming, 'Find something, and keep the TV on there! You don't have to change the channels every time there's a commercial!' When I go to sleep, I will smell the Gain in the sheets because you refused to wash laundry in anything else.

"You are everywhere I go. You will be a thought in everything that I eat. You are a constant, never ending memory. I can smell memories of you right now.

"And I'm supposed to watch you on the arm of some other nigga? I have been watching your belly grow with a baby that doesn't belong to me! My daughter is going to be sent off to prom by two men?! Another man is invading my space! He went where no man was supposed to go! And you let it happen!

"At our daughter's college graduation, I'm supposed to see you parade with another nigga?! All I know is to protect you! See about you. Check on you. Make sure you're okay. Ensure your safety. Provide for you. And I'm all of a sudden supposed to stop?

"I'm supposed to trust that somebody else who hasn't been around half the time that I've known you is going to do a good job at that? I'm supposed to rest knowing that a nigga you barely know now has that responsibility? I'm supposed to throw you to him like a football and pray that he don't fumble?

"A motherfucking piece of paper don't erase you! Them divorce papers don't make the memories and smell of you disappear. You are not forgotten just because I signed my name on a dotted line, Aniyah! I couldn't just sign the effervescence of you away.

"You are *still* my reason for living. Do you not get that? Do you not understand what love is? I. Love. You. You are my silver lining. My pot of gold at the end of the rainbow. My glass ceiling. I can't go no higher than you. It don't get no better than you. No one is for me, but you.

"I understand that it's over. But please take it easy on me. Remember what you have put me through. A quiet house is not peace; it is failure. And I will remember that I failed every time I put that key in the door and Ocean doesn't run up to me. I will have to drink my failure every time I look at my phone, and there is no corny joke from you. I am reminded that I'm not enough every time I look at you and see a baby who doesn't belong to me.

"Please, Aniyah. I know you have to live. I know that your life is now everything you have ever wanted. But for me, this is a nightmare that I cannot wake up from. If you don't see me as your husband anymore, please see me as a friend who has been more than there for you.

"If you see me as a friend, please—for the next few months—consider my pain, and don't joog the knife any deeper than it already is. Please. I am learning how to live and survive right now. My air is already gone. Don't turn up the heat. Please. Please. Please."

I wanted to feel guilty. I only ended up feeling guilty for not feeling guilty. I was not moved. I felt nothing towards him. I tried to muster up a tear because I felt that was supposed to happen during a time like that, but I couldn't even produce one tear out of one eye.

interVENTion

I did not want him. And I was so glad to be free. I hated that he was hurting. I knew that God would heal him in due time. But for that moment, he just had to hurt.

"I will not deepen the wound. Have a good day, Leonard."

I walked away. I heard the shackles fall off of my body. The chains fell to the ground. The rope was removed from my neck. I sincerely wanted him to find a good woman who loved and wanted him. Because she was not me.

interVENTion

Chapter 15

Lenny and Aniyah Now

inter~~VENT~~ion

"Hello?"

"Hey, Lenny. It's Aniyah."

"Niyah," he sighed, relieved. "I have been praying for you. I have been worried about you, Lady. Ocean told me that you can't have visitors. I tried calling you, but your phone is off, I guess. I would have come seen you or wrote you, but Ocean said that's not allowed, either. I've just... how are you?"

Tears fall down my face. Out of nowhere. I thought I was fine. Then I remembered that my son is not here. And he never will be. I am *here* because he isn't.

"Lenny, I am fine," I stifle my tears. "No, we can't have visitors outside of immediate family. We can't have personal phones because the people here monitor everything, making sure our environment remains conducive. Even this conversation is being recorded. But I am fine."

"No. You aren't fine. What can I do? Can I bring you something? You meet me at the front door? What are the rules? Damn the rules. I'll break them. What—"

"Leonard. I was calling to apologize for never apologizing to you."

The phone is completely silent now. I am fishing for the next words to say and the order to put them in. I think he is, too.

"I shouldn't have allowed divorce to be an option," I continue. "I should have gone to counseling like you said. I shouldn't have stepped outside of our vows. I shouldn't have been so careless with your feelings. I shouldn't have neglected being a wife to you. I shouldn't have allowed my heart to feel for another man. I was wrong. All the way wrong. And I am so sorry."

Silence.

"Are you here?" I ask him.

"Yeah," he rushes to say. "I'm here. And I hear you. What is all this about?"

"I'm not trying to come on to you or get back with you. I'm just trying to make peace with my demons and right all of my wrongs."

"I forgive you. You know, Aniyah, I needed you to hurt me. That pain made me grow up and man up. I had to see an empty house in order to realize that I was lacking. Providing financially wasn't enough. I needed to be a fucking man. For you. For Ocean. For myself. Going to counseling wasn't going to make me realize that. Only pain and sorrow could put me through that.

"Me and you—we spoke different languages. You spoke Survival and Hustle and Grind. I spoke Excuses and Regret. We didn't deserve each other. It just could not work. We both tried at some point. But we just wouldn't have ever been able to make it work.

inter~~VENT~~ion

"I thank God we got Ocean out of the
marriage, though. And I'm glad you're apologizing
now instead of then. Because you wouldn't have
meant it then. I know that you mean it now.

"And we both are finally happily married now.
We both grew up. We both got the people we really
wanted. And I finally got me a son.

"Oh, my God! I am so sorry, Aniyah. My bad.
I didn't mean—"

"You are good," I laugh. "It's all good. Thank
you for taking care of Ocean in my absence. She has
turned out to be a phenomenal young lady. Trel said
that she was Valedictorian, graduated high school
Summa Cum Lade. The list goes on and on. And I am
so happy you got a son. Ocean wasn't interested in
football at *all*."

"Naw, she wasn't," he laughs.

"I've missed so much with Ocean. So much
that I will *never* get back. Elementary graduation,
prom, first boyfriend, probably first something else,
high school graduation, first day of college, her
getting a driver's permit, driver's license. Does she
even have a job? Is she in college? What is she
majoring in? Who is she?"

"She goes to Spelman, and she is majoring in
biology. Our baby girl is going to be a pediatrician.
She works every other weekend at the sandwich shop
up the street from my house. It's just enough to put a

few hundred in her pocket. I pay her car note and car insurance. Hell, I pay every damn thang. All she gotta do is wake up and go to school.

"She is very distant, to herself, anti-social, and mysterious. To be honest, I don't know if the girl is gay or straight or neither. She has a wall up. It's been there ever since Elijah passed. And there is no getting over it, through it, under it, or around it. I have had her in therapy ever since Elijah passed. If she is like this with therapy, I'm scared to know how she would be without it.

"But she is very focused and determined. She's never not accomplished what she set out to do. She was Valedictorian, student of the year every year from sixth to twelfth grade. She got so many awards and medals in track and swimming. She is amazing. When her wall comes down, the world will really see it. Right now, the smoke screen is distorting her power."

"I don't know her at all," I cry. "How has ten years passed by?! How have I neglected my child?! I was so consumed with who wasn't here that I neglected who was. Ten years of accomplishments, accolades, awards. Accepted into an all Black female college?! My daughter is going to be a doctor?! What?!

"Karma don't forget, do she? I gave you so much hell during the divorce to not get custody of her, and you ended up with her anyway. I held on to her out of ugliness and spite, but she ended up away from me anyway. Karma didn't forget about me," I continue to cry.

"But you still have time, Aniyah. She ain't dead. You have time. There are other firsts that still haven't happened, yet. She hasn't gotten married. She hasn't had kids. She hasn't graduated college. She hasn't gotten her first real job. She hasn't opened up her own practice, yet.

"You can still be there. Start from today. And I will talk to her to make sure that she meets you halfway. I never bad-mouthed you to her. I did my best to explain to her that you were sick. I told her the same way people with stomach aches can't control their vomit, people with mental aches can't control the hurt that they cause people.

"I always let her know that it was nothing personal towards her, but it was personal within yourself. I believe that she will come around. Her pain is—she's a teenager. But I will keep talking to her. I will make sure she talks about this in therapy. I will make sure she acknowledges that you are trying. That you are doing what you need to do to be her mom again."

"Lenny. You are so awesome. Thank you. I gave you so many wounds, and here you are, healing mine."

"You gone always be my homie, Niyah. You know, there's a story in the Bible where people asked

Jesus who sinned, making the man blind. Was it him, his mom, or his dad? Who? And Jesus told them that no one sinned. That He allowed the man to be blind so that God's works could be displayed through the blind man and so that God could get the glory.

"Don't think that your son was born with a heart condition because you and Montrel sinned. Naw. It was so that God's works could be displayed, and it was for the glory of God. What Elijah had kills most kids before their first birthday. He made it to six years old with no symptoms. He had a goodl life. His life was full of life!

"He didn't suffer every day like other kids with his condition did. You didn't have to spend years watching your son die in agony. He didn't live six years taking pill after pill. He enjoyed his life. He lived more in six years than healthy people do in seventy five.

"He traveled the world. He spoke and understood three languages. He always had on the freshest kicks. He never went hungry. He didn't know what the word 'no' meant because his parents gave him the world.

"He left here knowing nothing but love and acceptance. He left here better than we will leave here. Think of all the bullshit we done been through while living. And we got a whole lot more bull shit coming our way if we have time left on this earth.

"Before we die, we would have experienced: rejection, embarrassment, belittlement, being lied on, being set up, divorce, abuse in every sense of the word, being cheated on, STDs, repossession, eviction, homelessness, hunger, being dead ass broke to where we couldn't even buy a stick of gum to curve our hunger pains, I've been shot by my step dad, and you have had to do what nobody should ever have to do—bury a child. I have not even named half the shit that we done experienced. And who knows what pain is left while we still here?

"But Elijah had the blessing of not experiencing any of it. That's God's works being displayed through Elijah's heart condition. That's God getting the glory through Elijah's heart condition and his death. Elijah never knowing pain is God getting the glory. God had His hands on him the entire time."

"I just wish we would've known. There is medicine for that that he could have been taking," I say.

"Elijah was too full of life to live according to it being time to take a pill. It wasn't going to work. He was hard-headed and stubborn. That wouldn't have been a desirable life for him. Only for you and Montrel.

"Aniyah, listen to me. Elijah lived all the days that God intended him to and not a day less. If God wanted Elijah to take pills, He would have revealed the condition to you. But He hid it until its appointed time so that He could get the glory. So that you would be able to know that God kept him alive, not pills."

"That, God did."

"I apologize for not getting you the help that you needed. I didn't know that it was that bad until about two years ago when you didn't show up to Ocean's graduation. Ocean told me that you couldn't come because you were taking Elijah somewhere, then it hit me. All at once.

"I knew that Trel was the one I talked to about Ocean all the time instead of you. I guess I was in denial. And I didn't know how to appropriately address the situation. Especially since you have a husband. I didn't want to overstep any boundaries or disrespect your marriage.

"I prayed for you. I prayed for God to heal you however He saw fit. I guess this is the way He saw fit.

"You are not crazy. Something like this is designed to break you. You cannot go through this untouched. It's supposed to hurt. If it didn't hurt, it couldn't heal. Just get up, feel it all, talk about whatever it is that you are feeling to whoever will listen, cry, and move on. Because he isn't coming back. But you have time left to live. Don't spend the rest of your life living just to be in sorrow.

inter~~inter~~VENT~~ion~~

"You are where you need to be. The help is there. Get it. You are there. You didn't go through all of this of being separated from Montrel and living in a strange place to not come out on top.

"I know you. You have pride. You are stubborn. You are strong-willed.

"During a time like this, it's easy for you to say: 'I ain't finna tell these folks my business.' 'I ain't finna let these people tell me what to do.' 'I'm grown.' 'I'm embarrassed.' 'I don't need to be here.'

"Aniyah, you gotta let that 'I' complex go. That 'I' mentality needs to shrink as small as you can get it. That 'I' needs to be as small as a sesame seed. In an intervention, the 'I' should always be small. You ain't gonna get nowhere with pride and shame.

"An inter**vent**ion is nothing if you don't **vent**. That's all intervention means: to **vent**, let it go, blow off that steam. **Vent**, Aniyah. Say the words. And let it go so that it will let go of you.

"**Vent**."

I crumble to the ground crying. An outpour of confusing emotions leave my core. I know that Lenny is right. I appreciate him. He didn't have to console me. He didn't have to stay on the phone with me. After all I did to him, he doesn't have to be so sweet and kind to me. I appreciate him more than he will ever know.

inter~~inter~~VENT~~ion~~

I just want my son back.

"And I also apologize for attacking your Blackness," Lenny continues. "I am a huge rider and supporter of Black people, and I believe in nurturing and sharpening us—not tearing us down. I said some bitter stuff to you the day you said you wanted a divorce.

"I was wrong to try to cause a divide with you in our community with my words. I was wrong to make you even look at yourself differently or question yourself. You *are* a Black woman. You have fought for so much change in our community. You have been a loud voice towards social injustices, double-sided tactics, unfair treatment, and the list goes on.

"I was no better than a Black person who is racist towards Black people. I said something about your light brown skin and 'good hair'. That is part of the problem in our community: instead of respecting a Black person as a Black person, we cause further division between us by labeling and categorizing each other according to how light skinned or dark we are, according to how well or rough we speak, according to the textures of our hair, according to where we grew up, etcetera.

"Black people need to look at other Black people and just have nothing but love for each other. We need to look at another Black person and respect the struggle. Because truth is, even though Black people look at you and see light brown skin and 'good hair', White folks look at you and see a nigger. They don't see no difference in you and me. I see light brown, they just see brown. So, you definitely know the struggle.

"I was mad. I was hurt. I was pissed. But I was wrong. I crossed the line. Honestly, you probably have it harder being a biracial Black woman trying to prove her Blackness than I have being a one hundred percent Black man. I'm sorry."

"I forgive you. It's all good between me and you. But you have no idea the pain of being *almost* White," I laugh.

"Gahdamn," he laughs back.

"I *almost* had a seat at the table. I *almost* had some of that good ole White privilege. I *almost* arrived. I *almost* had it made. Had nine toes in the door before they slammed it in my face. I *almost* made it."

"For real though, Niyah, I'm glad that *almost* doesn't count. You and I have made some good contributions to our community. We got some laws changed, new books put into schools' curriculums… I don't know if your drive would have been that strong if you had a seat at the table.

"I'm also glad that after our divorce, we still remained friends. God so good that me and your husband are friends. We became friends when Elijah was what? Three months old when Trel needed me to babysit Elijah and his other son while you and him protested some injustice.

"Me and Trel still hang all the time. We always got the kids together while you… regrouped. And you know that all four of us took our kids on trips together when Elijah was here. God is just good like that.

"I miss you, Aniyah. I'm ready for you to be you again. I miss you out here marching and protesting. When you get back to you, I want to be beside you outside the court house when you are back to picketing injustices like we did when Elijah was alive. I'm out here still marching, and people always ask me about you. Me and Montrel protested in Dallas a year ago when Botham Jean was murdered by that White cop for being Black in his own apartment, and everybody asked us, 'Where is Aniyah?'

"You are one of our faces that everybody looks for. No one has forgotten about you. Don't you forget about you, either. **Vent**, and get back to you. **Vent**, and get back to *us*—Black people. You still have a purpose on your life that you need to live out and fulfill. Your family and community still need you. You still need you."

interVENTion

Chapter 16

Can't "*And*"

"How often do you think about drinking?" Mr. Brite asks me during Group.

"I can't believe it, but only once a day now. I never had to think about drinking because I was already drinking. Then when I first got here, there was not a second that went by that tequila wasn't on my mind. Now, I'm down to thinking about tequila once a day. I never thought I'd see this day."

"What changed it?"

"Crazy enough—excuse me for using the word 'crazy'—strangely enough, being sober cleared out my thought processes to where I realize being intoxicated just ain't doing it for me. It has gotten me nowhere. I couldn't realize that when I was always sloppy drunk. My perception isn't distorted now. I just almost don't want it anymore."

"So that one time a day that you want to drink. Why?"

"Out of habit and wanting to hold on to what is familiar. My world is changing so fast. My ex-husband and I held a conversation with each other for the first time in about eight years. Because I'm not drinking anymore, I'm losing weight and looking different. The stress of waking up every morning at four to take care of someone who doesn't exist is now gone, so I'm looking younger.

"I also realize that I can't drink because I am actually taking my meds, and I really want to take my meds. Alcohol and psych meds do not mix. Which is one reason why I never took the meds— because I didn't want to stop drinking. But part of my healing is taking meds that are keeping me stabilized and level-headed. With being stabilized and level-headed, I'm now able to realize that my son Elijah Thomas Brent is dead.

"My head is spinning from all this new stuff. So, I want to hold onto *something* familiar. And there is nothing more familiar than an Amaretto Sour on the rocks."

The group begins clapping for me.

"What did I do?" I ask.

"You said it. You said that your son is dead. You have been here for over a month, and you have never been able to say it. That is a huge milestone for you. Congratulations!" Mr. Brite says.

I let that soak in. I have *never* said that. I have *never* admitted that. Oh, my God. God, thank you. It's a start.

My son Elijah Thomas Brent is dead.

My son Elijah Thomas Brent is dead.

My son Elijah Thomas Brent is dead.

The freedom that comes with the truth. The truth really does make you free. I haven't accepted it, yet, but I can say it. It's a start. And I will keep going.

interVENTion

I want to be healed. I want to be whole. There is no such thing as half way healed or partly sick. You are either sick or healed; there is no in between. There is no such thing as healing a part of me and letting another part be sick. I can't be healed *and* drunk. I can't be healed *and* bitter. I can't be healed *and* in denial. I am giving up a lot just for one goal: to be healed.

"I drank for the first time when I was fifteen," I blurt out.

The room is looking at me. My palms are sweating. My voice is trembling. My chest is pounding.

"Mr. Argustar, my first day in Group you asked me what made me drink."

"Yes, I did."

"I want to be healed so bad," I cry.

"Then **vent**," Mr. Argustar tells me.

"I was fifteen, in the tenth grade, and I was dating the All American football player from high school. He was a freshman in college, and he always sported me on his arm. I mean, I was blessed that someone like him wanted me. I was short, chubby, pimply-faced, awkward. But he wanted me.

"We had been dating for about a year and a half. He invited me over to his friend's house because his friend's parents weren't home, and he wanted to just... *chill* with me without interruptions. I innocently went over there.

"Within five minutes of me being there, he had me pinned down on a washing machine with one hand sinking into my chest while his other hand ripped my panties off. I was screaming for help, and his friend just turned the music up. The louder I screamed, the louder his friend turned the music up.

"It felt like an army tank was unsuccessfully trying to find a parking spot inside of me over and over again, and it didn't give up until the gear went out. My tears didn't stop him. My screams didn't slow him down. He stopped when *he* was finished.

"I walked home in the dark with blood trickling down my legs. I replayed the scene so many times in my head, wondering what I could have done to prevent it. I realized that it was my fault because I went over there knowing no adults would be home, and I had on a skirt. I must have been asking for it. It was my fault.

"It hurt to move. My vagina was so tender and sore and just...mutilated it felt like. I remembered my uncle always talking about alcohol being a pain killer. So, I drunk the alcohol just to get out of physical pain. I didn't know that it also drowned mental and spiritual pain, too. But I soon found that out.

"I couldn't talk to anybody about it because I had convinced myself that it was my fault. I couldn't tell my mama that I went over a boy's house in a skirt without adult supervision. I surely couldn't tell my brothers because they would have killed him. My dad was killed when I was six, so I couldn't tell him.

"I had no one except Hennessy. No matter the time of day, he listened. He was there whenever I called. My mom drank a lot so she didn't notice that the bottles were emptying out. She just assumed that she was drinking them that fast.

"And one day after six months or so, the pain of the rape didn't hurt anymore—physically, mentally, or spiritually. So, I stopped drinking. I never sought help or talked to anyone about it. I just woke up okay one day.

"I believed it was my fault for twelve years— which is part of the reason why I never told anyone. I never even called it a rape. I called it sex.

"Even though I told him no, I still thought it was sex. I didn't know that my 'no' held weight. I thought it was a suggestion that he could choose or not choose to honor. He chose not to. I thought I had to be okay with that."

"What changed your mind after twelve years? What made you realize that it wasn't sex? What happened to make you understand that he violated you?" Mr. Argustar asks me.

"I had my daughter. I looked down at her for the first time, and I saw her innocence, her youth, her naivete. The first thought that I had was that I have to protect that with my life. And nobody—male or female—will ever do to her what that bastard did to me.

"My daughter became my reason to live when I twenty-seven years old, and she's my reason to live again at forty-six years old. I failed her once, but I will not fail her again."

Chapter 17
Zebra

"Thank you for coming to see me today, Babe."

"Of course, Niyah."

"Today is the tenth anniversary of Elijah's death," I tell Trel.

His eyes buck. I guess he forgot.

"You forgot?" I ask him.

"No, Babe. Never. I just never heard you say it. I've never heard you say that Elijah is dead."

"I've been saying it a lot lately."

His face is showing that there is so much that he wants to say, but he doesn't know what will hurt or help, so he says nothing at all.

"I had Sour Patch Kids today," I laugh.

"All you did was suck the sour off and throw the candy away."

"And now the roof of my mouth is toe up!"

"You never learn," he laughs.

"It's soooo good," I croon.

"I got something to tell you something that I never told you," Trel tells me.

"Okay?"

"I had known you for a while, ya know? You were my accountant and shit like that. When we decided to be official, you had me to come over and meet your mom. When she opened that door, I shit a brick!"

"Why?" I ask Trel.

"In all those years of us kicking it, you forgot tell me that your mama is White!"

I pause and think about it. He is so right. I never thought to tell him that; it never seemed important or necessary.

Laughing, I say, "Oh! That! Yea. My mama is White."

"No shit, Sherlock! It never even crossed my mind that you had anybody in your family that was White! Especially not a parent! Me and you sat up all the time talking about the social injustices on Blacks and Browns. You were always talking about buying Black, recreating Black Wall Street, building the Black communities. You spent so much of your time marching and protesting in these streets. You ain't sound like you had no White in you at all.

"And you know my family don't do White people. At all. And here I am in this White woman's living room, getting ready to eat her food. The whole time at her house, I was praying, 'God, I repent for what I did. Please forgive me. Please save me. I've spent my whole life fighting for the Black and Brown people. Don't let me go like this. The story can't end like this. If you let me out of this house alive, I swear I will never look back. I will leave this pretty, curly headed, Black girl alone. I swear, God. Please spare me.' "

"So, what happened to that promise? Because I don't recall you ever leaving me alone."

"I kept that promise from the time I walked out of your mama's house until I drove to the stop sign by her house."

I laugh so hard that tears form.

"You laughing, Aniyah, but that was the longest six seconds of my life. I was serious about leaving your ass alone. I was just gone raise our son, but stop fooling with you like that. But when I got to that stop sign, I looked in my rearview mirror, and you were getting mail out the mailbox. I said, 'God, she's so damn pretty. She's so damn thick. She bakes like nobody else. She's so down to earth. She's so damn cool. God, I can't leave her alone. I'm ready for whatever.' "

"I remember you just sitting at that stop sign. I figured somebody had paged you or something."

"Naw. I was just sitting there, risking it all. Then I had to go to my parents' house and tell them."

"I never thought about that! Your parents hate White people! How did that go? What did you say?"

"I said, 'Madre. Padre. You remember Aniyah?' They said they did. I said, 'Well, she's Black.' They looked at me like *duh*. I said, 'And her mom is light skinned.' They were nodding their heads, not giving a damn. Then I said, 'Aniyah's mom's parents are White. That makes Aniyah's mom White.'

"My dad flew out of his chair. 'Of all the gotdamn girls you could have chosen! You chose a zebra! I didn't fight in wars, serve in the military, sacrifice my time away from my family, miss y'all growing up just so that your dumb ass can get me killed!'

"And my mama: 'Mijo. You no think. Y'all's kids will have a White grandmother. No good, Mijo! Dangerous! Why you no think?!'

"My parents can't speak or understand English, but they spoke perfect English that day! That day, I almost gave my parents a stroke. I couldn't get them to understand why I took a fruit off the Tree of Life. I told them I *just* found out that your mom was White.

"They said now that I know, leave you alone. Abort the child. And move on with life. I couldn't dare. I would never. I knew you were worth whatever came with the situation. I felt like that then. I feel like that now. You are my Achilles heel, Aniyah."

"I'm sorry, Trel. She'd been my mama my whole life. Her being White never stuck out to me as pertinent information. I don't think of her as my White mama. She's my mama. The dots never connected when you would talk about how much you can't stomach White people. I have my own issues with them myself. I love them, but they don't love me.

"I have never passed for anything except Black. My hair is kinky-curly. I'm light brown—but brown, nevertheless. I have wide hips. Wide nose. I dance on rhythm. Nothing about me reminds me that there is another piece to the puzzle. I'm seriously sorry for not giving you the heads up."

"I forgive you for having a White mama," he smirks.

"How is your son? How is Lucas?" I ask Trel.

"Lucas is twenty-one, a mechanic, married, and a dad."

My body begins to go limp.

"What? We're grandparents?"

"Yea. To twins. Monte and Aliviah. They're five. It was a big fight between us when he was fifteen, telling me he was about to be a dad. Then, when he was sixteen, they were born, and I forgot that I was even mad."

"Have I met them?"

Trel silently shakes his head "no".

"Didn't want the babies around the crazy lady?" I asked, talking about myself.

"We just wanted the babies as safe as possible."

"I totally get it. He's married to their mom?"

"Oh yea. They are twins they damn self. One can't move without the other. When you see Lucas, you see Shameka."

"Shameka? Lucas got him a sista?"

"Hell yea. I raised him right!"

We both raise our Black power fists and laugh.

"And what about your ex-wife Lavender?"

"She still hates me. We ain't got the fairytale ending like you and Lenny. Hell, me and Lavender ain't got the fairytale ending like me and Lenny. She hates my guts, and every time something goes bad in my life, she throws a party. But that's what I get for not marrying a sista the first time."

"You married a sista the second time, and it didn't work well for you, Montrel."

"That's because I failed you. It was nothing that you did. I didn't want nobody calling you crazy or even saying that if I was a good husband, you wouldn't have lost your mind. I was so worried about what people would say and how they would look at us. I put peoples' views and opinions above your mental health, and I am sorry."

"A lot of people failed me these past ten years, Montrel. Not just you."

"But I'm the one who took the vow to never hurt you. You have *my* last name. You are mine to protect. I fumbled the ball. I just thank God that you are here to recover."

Chapter 18

P.S., I'm Sorry

inter~~VENT~~ion

    I was supposed to had written Ocean a letter a long time ago, but the words just don't ever seem to come out right. What can I say? What can be said? How do I erase ten years of pain and neglect? I chose depression over her. How do I apologize?

Dear Ocean,

~~How are you?~~

~~Hey, Baby Girl.~~

~~I heard you attend Spelman now.~~

~~Your dad told me that you run track.~~

~~You are an introvert like me I hear.~~

~~What is your favorite color?~~

~~How tall are you?~~

~~When is your birthday?~~

~~I've never personally known a pediatrician.~~

~~Is your hair relaxed or natural?~~

~~What color are your eyes?~~

~~Do you have a southern accent like me?~~

~~Do people still say "Decatur where it's greater"?~~

~~Whether you like men or women doesn't matter to me. You are my child, and I love you.~~

~~Are you transgender?~~

~~I miss you.~~

~~The food here sucks.~~

~~They walk us for an hour every day like we are dogs.~~

~~I want a kitten when I come home.~~

~~Would you like to live with me? I don't mind.~~

~~I just want to get to know you for myself.~~

~~What is your favorite song?~~

~~Who is your favorite artist?~~

~~I wanted to be a writer when I was in high school until I found out what "starving artist" really means.~~

~~I think about you all day every day.~~

~~You are Black Girl Magic.~~

~~"I'm doing this for you. Whenever I want to quit, I think about you. You are my inspiration and motivation to get better."~~

~~Please tell your therapist that I am doing my part now.~~

inter~~inter~~VENT~~ion~~

~~Please forgive me.~~

~~Please accept me into your life.~~

~~Let's heal together.~~

I'm sorry.

Aniyah Brent,

Your mom

Chapter 19

INTERVENTION

inter~~VENT~~ion

"Hey, Daughter," my mama smiles at me.

"Hey, Mommy."

She sighs and stares at me across the table at my visitation. Her words are playing hop scotch in her mind. She's jumping and fumbling and doubling back over words. She wants to be careful in what she says; she also wants to be effective. She doesn't know where the line between the two are.

"I've been here before, you know? In a facility like this," Mama says. "As a matter of fact, I've been here six times. Each time was because I couldn't handle the thought of having to had bury a child. And I ended up burying three.

"You are not crazy, Aniyah. You are human. This shit hurts. *Nobody* is built for this—the death of a child. No one can handle that and go to work the next day. No one is supposed to bury a child. Whatever you are feeling, whatever your thoughts— you're supposed to have them. No matter what they may be. No one who has never been in your shoes can judge you."

I let out a scream. A long, deep, ear piercing scream. I release it. I let it go. The pain, shortness of breath, mental anguish, heaviness in my chest—I let it all out. I release it to the atmosphere and let the air decide what it wants to do with it. I can't be the owner of it anymore.

inter~~VENT~~ion

My mom never budges. She looks as calm as she did when she sat down. She remains sitting at the visitor's table, waiting on me to finish. She is giving me time.

I have time to grieve.

"He's dead," I whisper to her with my hand full of my hair. "Elijah is dead."

"Sweetie. He is. My grandson is dead. I have a hole in my heart, too. We can get through this torment together."

She hands me a journal with a curly headed plus size Black woman on it. The woman looks like me.

"When I was in here, pen and paper were my best friends. All the things that you don't want anyone to hear or know, write it in here. It doesn't have to make sense. Just get it out of your system," she tells me.

"Mommy. This woman on the front of this diary looks like me."

"I know. That's why I got it."

I am speechless. My mom has never—in my forty six years of life—acknowledged that I am Black. She always bought me White dolls. She relaxed my hair at four years old because she didn't like the way my hair looked. She bleached my hair blonde and made me wear blue contacts from the time

I was fourteen to eighteen to get me as close to White as possible. She never let me play outside for fear of me getting darker. My being Black was always a pink elephant in the room. Without my expectation, she addressed the pink elephant today.

"You recognize that I am Black?" I ask her.

Sighing with her eyes closed, she answers, "Yes. I've only birthed Black kids."

"You've never acted like you knew that we are Black."

"Aniyah, I have never had a problem with my children being Black. I had children with the darkest man in the world. I knew that I was going to have Black children. Your being Black was never the problem. The problem was that you didn't look like me. None of my kids do. All of you are brown. And I am Casper.

"We would go to the stores, and people would look at me like I didn't belong. Like y'all were in a league, and I was the chaperone. Like y'all were a team, and I was the coach. No one ever looked at y'all and looked at me and thought that we were a family. I have never felt that I belonged. The whole house could relate to each other, and I was on the sidelines praying for the coach to let me in. And the coach never did.

"And you were especially different because I couldn't relate to you on *any* level after I knew that we would have a common ground. When I found out that you were going to be a girl, I thought, 'Finally. Finally, I will have a child that I can identify with.' You were a girl. My only girl, and I was so excited when I found out I was finally having a girl. My sixth attempt finally got me a girl.

"You were already brown, so I couldn't relate to you there. But I just knew that we could relate on feminine things. I was wrong. You were a tomboy. You loved the streets. I knew nothing about the streets! You wouldn't wear make-up. You wouldn't put a purse on your shoulders. I couldn't pay you to wear a dress. Heels were not even in the question.

"I loved sewing; you loved basketball. I loved soap operas; you loved video games. You loved dolls, but you wanted them to look like you. Looking like you meant not looking like me.

"You were supposed to be my golden child because you are a girl. But you weren't. You blended right on in with your dad and brothers. You *were* a disappointment to me. But not because you were Black. Because you didn't live up to the feminine expectations that I placed on you when you were in my womb.

"I wanted to be able to relate to all of my kids. I wanted us to all look alike so that I would feel like we were a family. Whether that meant I got darker or y'all got lighter, I wanted us to look like a family. I tanned so that I would become brown, and I tried to keep y'all in the house so that you wouldn't get darker. No matter how much I tanned and kept y'all in the house, our colors never met in the middle.

"I just wanted us to look like we were a family. And I still do. Don't you look like your daughter? How would you feel if you didn't? I don't look like my grandkids, either. I'm in a world by myself. A world that I put myself in, but it still hurts."

"You felt like you didn't belong?! I felt like I didn't belong! I remember plenty of times going out with you, and people would look at you with a star in their eyes, then they would look at me, and say, 'Ugh.' You were so pretty and perfect, and you had me—a dark spot—dragging alongside you. I was constantly being compared to you by strangers. Their looks always reminded me that I was just a nigger."

"Don't you say that!" she yells as she stands and hits the table. "I have met plenty of those, and they were all *White!* I did not marry nor birth anything but intelligent, powerful, and influential royalty. I don't care how they looked at you! I know what you are. I always have."

"Mommy, you put chemicals on my hair to straighten it every six weeks from the time that I was four years old. Then when I turned fourteen, you bleached it blonde. My hair fell out plenty of times because it couldn't handle a relaxer and being bleached. You made me wear blue contacts. You always did something to make me look different than what God made me. From the beginning of time, you made me feel that I had to be fixed. That what God placed on my head is a disgrace that I should be ashamed of."

"I knew nothing about Black people's hair, Aniyah. I didn't know what to do with it. I had no idea how to style it. I did that to make it easier on myself."

"Making it easier on yourself made me not know myself! Why didn't you research how to comb your daughter's hair instead of transforming her into something that she wasn't?! You made me feel like I had to change to be valuable. I was thirty-four years old when I realized that my hair was not a curse!"

She silently gasps, right hand over her chest. "I am so sorry," she cries. "That was never my intention, Aniyah. *Never*. I just didn't know what to do with a Black girl. I didn't know. Please don't punish me for not knowing."

"Your not knowing punished *me*."

"Aniyah."

"At forty-six, I'm still trying to undo what you did. And I don't think I ever can. Me and my brothers would come home, telling you of what we endured at school as Black kids. The obvious racism from our White teachers. The bullying from our White classmates. And you just brushed it off every time. You were *never* our defender or protector."

"Y'all wanted me to hate my people!"

"Your *children* are your people! And we didn't want you to hate them; we wanted you to see how they hated *us*!"

"Ani—"

"You didn't want to see it! Your own husband—my dad—was gunned down by the police while sleeping in his own car doing nothing but waiting on you to come out the store! He was unarmed. The car was off. The windows were up. His eyes were closed. And the cop got off with saying that he thought my dad had a gun pointed at him.

"You did *nothing*! Nothing while the cop never even got suspended. They were so happy that he got another nigger off the streets that he got promoted to detective. You cared nothing about the problems of *your children's* people.

"I was an orphan in my own home with my *biological* mom. You created a childhood for me that I have been trying to heal from for forty-six years. Rejection raised me. Pain molded me. Neglect nurtured me. And people wonder how I ended up in a facility like this. **YOU** put me here!

"*You* were the start of my mental illness. I was mentally unstable long before Elijah died. I was mentally unstable long before I had kids. *You* made me crazy. You broke me.

"And I wasn't healed from anything you did to me when I got married. I wasn't healed from anything

you did to me when I started my business. I wasn't
healed from anything you did to me when I had
Ocean. I wasn't healed from anything you did to me
when I had Elijah. I wasn't healed from anything you
did to me when I got divorced. I wasn't healed from
anything you did to me when I got married for a
second time. I wasn't healed from anything you did to
me when my son died. Sitting in front of you, I'm *still*
not healed from anything you did to me.

"That is why everything I have touched has
failed. I have been operating in pain my whole
fucking life! Pain that you have given me. Pain that
you handed me with a smile on your face.

"I don't need an intervention with my son's
death. I need an intervention with all that shit you put
me through! You made me live a life of suppressing
and hiding and covering who I was. You made me
live every day denying who I was. And when I would
try to be me, I got punished.

"You punished me for being Black long
before the world did. You hated me before the world
did. You fucked me up so good that the only thing
that could break me again was my son dying. There
was no other pain that I could feel.

"You missed the opportunity to be my mom.
You missed the opportunity to raise me. You missed
the opportunity to build a bond with me. And I
repeated the same fucked up cycle with my daughter.

inter~~VENT~~ion

"My son being dead is not what has me in here. Not being healed from you is!"

I walk away from the visitor's table with the diary. I go into my room, find a pen, curl up in my bed, and open the journal. I begin to **vent** with my pen:

The intervention between me and my Mom is making the intervention between me and my son's death possible. My habit of holding on to hurt and the impossible has died. Letting go of the unrealistic expectations that my mom placed on me has made room for me to let go of the unrealistic expectations that I have placed on my son—being alive.

I know that if I can walk away from the pain that she caused me, I can walk away from the pain that I have caused myself. If I can walk away from the pain of him not being here, I can walk away from all the pain and torture that she has caused me. In some way that I don't understand, leaving one situation makes leaving the other situation possible.

I guess I finally want to be free. Of every fucking thing. Free from the pain of being an unapologetic Black woman who was raised by a narcissistic White woman and free from taking care of a dead sixteen year old. My mind hurts. My heart is crumbled. I have to let it all go. Letting one go made it ok to let the other one go.

I'm taking Lenny's advice: I'm letting my mama's unrealistic expectations of me go so that the

interVENTion

unrealistic expectation of me will let me go. And with it letting me go, I am able to let the unrealistic expectation of my son being alive go.

I know it doesn't make sense. It doesn't have to. I'm just glad that it's happening. Thank you, Diary for being the intervention between me and my mama. You have allowed a forty-six year old overdue conversation to be had. Thank you for healing me. Now that I am healed of the pain my mama caused me, I can let my son go.

Thank you, Diary for this intervention.

Chapter 20

Camera

"Mrs. Brent. Are you ready?" Dr. White asks me.

I look in the mirror, exhale, and apprehensively confidently say, "Yes, Ma'am. Let's go."

We get on the facility's van and head to the cemetery. To see my son. To see Elijah. I am on the facility's van to see a tombstone with my son's name, date of birth…

….and date of death on it.

I'm not ready. I can't do this. I thought I could, but I can't.

"Dr. White!" I scream.

She jumps and looks at me. The van driver screeches to the side of the road, stopping, not knowing what is going on. They both look at me, and I am ready to turn around and go back to the facility. Then my and Lenny's conversation ring back to me: *Cry and move on. Don't dedicate the rest of my life to sorrow. It's supposed to hurt. If it didn't hurt, it couldn't heal.*

I want to feel the pain. I will not drink anything to numb the sting. If I can feel it, that means I'm alive. If I numb it, I will never feel it. If I never feel it, I will never heal from it.

I want it to heal.

inter~~VENT~~ion

For good this time.

"Did you bring the camera? I forgot to remind you before we left," I say to Dr. White, making it seem as if that is why I screamed.

"I did, Aniyah. It's right here," she says, showing me the camera.

"Ok. Mr. Joe, you can keep driving. I'm sorry. I got scared that I wouldn't have any tangible memories of this moment. But she remembered her camera."

Mr. Joe begins driving.

I think about all the people I could do this with: Montrel, Ocean, my mom, my siblings, my friends. Even Lenny. But I chose to do it alone. They would console me if they came. They would say things to make the pain go away. They would make me feel okay.

But I don't want to feel okay. I don't want the pain to go away. I want to feel every drop of ache that I have cut off for the past ten years.

I want to heal.

I have to follow Dr. White as she leads me to his gravesite—*Elijah's* gravesite—because I've never been here after the burial, and I have no idea how to get there. I didn't even know what cemetery he was in until now. Montrel showed her where to go in the beginning of my treatment.

inter~~VENT~~ion

And here we are.

Elijah Thomas Brent

December 24, 2003- January 6, 2010

Whether I live or die, I am the Lord's

Romans 14:8

I do what comes naturally to me. I lay on his gravesite. For me, it's symbolic to me holding him, lying next to him like we did every night until he went to sleep. Oh, how I miss holding and lying next to him. How I miss watching him sleep. How I miss him.

I rub every letter and read every word to make it real to me. I want to accept it this time. I swallow every morsel of agony and invite more in. This is the last time I want to feel this level of hurt, so I take it all in. I leave no grief on the table. I own it all. I welcome every negative feeling into my space so that I can give them all to God. I leave nothing behind.

I don't stifle my tears. I let them flow. I don't muffle my screams. The next street over hears me. I don't get up. I lay there until I can't lay no more. I shift positions to buy more time. And when I'm ready, I kiss the gravestone.

"Hey, Eli. It's Mommy. I have missed you so much. I miss that wild, untamable, curly, light brown hair. I miss your mischievousness. I miss your pranks. I miss your jokes. I miss you, Son.

"I have not been right since you… since you died. And I never will be the same. It's a permanent burn that I will always feel. But I will make peace with that burn. I will have joy again. I will give God the glory for all that *He* allowed you to overcome and survive.

"I still have a lot of questions that I may never get the answers for while on Earth. But one thing I do know is that you have an eternal, everlasting healing. There is no more sickness where you are. No more shortness of breath. No more passing out. You can't die again. You are *now* living the life. Enjoy your eternal rest, peace, and love. We will meet again."

My denial gave up the ghost and died. Never to return. I'm so grateful for that because she ain't welcomed here no more. I spent too many years with her. I'm ready to live with Acceptance and Peace.

interVENTion

Chapter 21

Bienvenido, Chica

inter~~VENT~~ion

"Welcome home, Baby!"

Montrel plows into me with a hug, and I have to stabilize myself before I fall back onto the floor.

"Thank you," I laugh.

LaTrice, Ocean, and my mom are waving banners, welcoming me in.

"I missed you guys so much. Oh, my gosh. I have missed you, Ocean. Not just these past six weeks. But for the last ten years. I have missed you."

"I have missed you, too, Mommy," Ocean says, hugging me.

"I am so sorry," I begin. "Ocean, you needed a mama. I wasn't there."

"Mommy, I've been going to counseling ever since I was nine years old. I forgive you. And I understand. You had nothing left in you to give. You can't pour from an empty cup. I am not mad anymore. And I got your letter. That's all I wanted—an apology."

I hug her as tight as she can stand it. "I felt guilty for being a mom to you when I couldn't be a mom to Elijah. I chose to not be a mom because if I couldn't mother all of my children, I wasn't going to mother any of them. I know that sounds stupid. I know it wasn't right or fair. I can't explain it. But that's how I felt."

Ocean replies, "I felt guilty for being with you when Elijah couldn't. I felt guilty for eating when he couldn't. I haven't eaten pizza in ten years because that was his favorite food, and I felt guilty for eating it when he couldn't. I felt guilty for going to school when he couldn't go anymore. I felt guilty for hanging with friends when he couldn't. I felt guilty for being alive, Mama. And I'm not sure if that guilt will ever go way."

It never hit me that my other child was going through pain and sorrow just like me. She went through all of this in silence. She went through all of this with my absence. She was just nine years old when he died, and she had to feel whatever she felt without her mommy.

What have I done?

We could have gone through it together. We could have explored her emotions together. We could have cried together. We could have healed together.

"Baby, the place where Elijah is has never ending pepperoni pizza. You better eat up!"

She genuinely laughs.

I grab her face and talk into her soul. "You are alive because God said so. Don't ever feel guilty or apologize for what God has done for you. You have so many decades left on this earth. Don't spend them in despair. Don't put yourself in a position where you look back and wonder where have the years gone.

Today, you and I are going to start living, and we are going to do life together. Okay?"

"Yes, Ma'am."

"And LaTrice—"

"Aniyah," she puts her hand up, stopping me, "*I* am sorry. *I* was in the wrong. As your best friend, I should have been gotten you the help that you needed long before now. I am more guilty than you are. You ended up in that place because I was silent.

"I was not your friend. Friends care about their friends' mental health. Friends have those awkward conversations with each other. I failed you. Don't you dare apologize to me. I am apologizing to you. I am so sorry, Aniyah. I am so sorry," she cries on my shoulder.

"You owe me a pack of Sour Patch Kids," I joke with her.

She reaches in her bra and pulls out a pack.

"I gotchu, Boo. You ain't gonna catch me slippin' again."

I snatch the bag from her and hug her. Instead of hugging me back, she holds me, rocks me, and nurtures me.

"When I see Lyric, I am going to apologize to her and make it up to her some kind of way. I am her Godmom. I owe her so much."

"She already forgives you. You just owe her your time."

My mom taps me on my back. We haven't talked since my visitation. I don't know what she wants, but I will listen. I will not ignore her the way she ignored me my entire life.

"I am proud of you," she begins. "I have birthed one brilliant *Black* woman with kinky-curly hair, caramelized skin, a wide nose, bowed hips, thick lips, and a rhythm that I would pay to have. I am so grateful that you are mine. I am so grateful that you are back."

I am so grateful to be back.

inter~~VENT~~ion

TIDBITS FROM THE AUTHOR

The book is titled inter<u>VENT</u>ion because of the intervention between Aniyah and her mom. Once that situation was resolved, Aniyah was able to let her son go.

My goal was to highlight the ineffective approaches and treatment to mental illness in the Black community as well as the Christian community.

My other goal was to show the effect of going through ANYTHING drastic can have on a marriage. I wanted to show the importance of going through things TOGETHER as a married couple. When storms come, separating is not the answer.

Aniyah wasn't able to admit or even say that her son was dead until she spoke with her ex-husband. As many wounds as she had given him, he was the one who helped her heal the most.

It is perfectly fine to have Jesus AND a therapist.

IN ORDER TO BE HEALED, YOU HAVE TO PUT ALL OF YOU ON THE OPERATING TABLE.

inter<u>VENT</u>~~ion~~

THANK YOU FOR READING! PLEASE LEAVE A REVIEW ON AMAZON.COM, GOODREADS, ETC.

PLEASE TELL PEOPLE ABOUT ME!

AUTOGRAPHED BOOKS AVAILABLE ON JHORDYNN.COM

FOLLOW JHORDYNN ON FACEBOOK: JHORDYNN

FOLLOW JHORDYNN ON INSTAGRAM: jhordynn_writes

SUBSCRIBE TO JHORDYNN'S YOUTUBE: JHORDYNN

SUBSCRIBE TO JHORDYNN'S WEBSITE: JHORDYNN.COM

NEED HELP WRITING A BOOK OR ANYTHING ELSE? MY COMPANY MADE 4 THIS CAN HELP YOU. CALL 318-406-2249, OR EMAIL YOUR QUESTIONS AND NEEDS TO BEASTEINC@GMAIL.COM

www.ingramcontent.com/pod-product-compliance
Lightning Source LLC
Chambersburg PA
CBHW020644250626
47154CB00008B/2799